The Part-1 Dictionary

riting and Pronunciation (spelled in English) of
Traditional Chinese Characters with

Radical Index Stroke No. 1 - No. 2
plus
Radical-Characters

鄭淑真

JANE S. J. LIN

Printed in Taiwan, Republic of China

For information address:

Elephant White Cultural Enterprise Ltd. Press,

8F.-2, No.1, Keji Rd., Dali Dist., Taichung City 41264, Taiwan (R.O.C.)

Distributed by Elephant White Cultural Enterprise Co., Ltd.

ISBN: 978-626-7151-73-0

Suggested Price: **NT$200**

Preface

This book (Part-One of Twelve) is the printouts from the databases that I designed for *Ez2Vital Software Inc.* – the company my husband Tim H. C. Lin, Ph.D. and I co-founded in 2005. Before the software is released, this book can be referenced for writing and pronouncing the Traditional Chinese characters with Stroke No. 1 and 2 listed on Radical Index. As for the meanings in English, please refer to "Pin-Yin" Chinese-English dictionaries on the markets. However, for the Mandarin speakers, it may require to lookup a Chinese dictionary to obtain the spellings in English for the character before looking up "Pin-Yin" Chinese-English Dictionary.

When Part One – Part Twelve all are published, the online software will include nearly 10,000 Traditional Chinese characters. As mentioned in the *Preface* of the "pioneering" edition, it is designed for writing traditional Chinese characters with correct stroke-sequences (starting with radical-characters) and multiple ways of spelling for pronunciation (starting with Last Names and radical-characters). Also, by applying the same idea for a "Plural-Surname" – a Last Name with more than one character, building words / idioms / phrases with as many as characters is also included my database design. In addition, the creation of the editions for any other languages is possible with a little effort.

I am enclosing the printout of the *Ez2Vital Software Inc.*'s *Home* page for introduction of the software and the revised **Preface** from the "pioneering" edition published in March 2022 for why and how I develop the databases.

鄭淑真

Jane S. J. Lin

April 2022
Pasadena, California, USA

Software Development
Database & Website Design
IT Services

Ez2Vital Software Inc.

Science Technology Engineering Art
Mathematics Workshop / Seminar /
Events / Class / Tutoring

| Home | About Us | Our Mission | Our Team | Wish List | Bulletin Board | Contact Us | Group Member Login |

An Unprecedented, Intelligent, Convenient, and Useful Tool

1. Nearly 10,000 Traditional Chinese Characters with the information:
1.1 The pronunciation (spelled in English) including multiple ways of Pin Yin (spelled by sound).
1.2 Its Radical Index – Radical Stroke Number and Sequence Number within the Radical Stroke Number.
1.3 Stroke-by-Stroke writings for its Radical and additional strokes.
1.4 The meanings in English.

2. Thousands of Words/Phrases/Idioms (formed from 1.) with the information:
2.1 The pronunciation Character-by-Character.
2.2 The meanings in English including the translation of Chinese.

3. The function of English-Chinese / Chinese-English Dictionaries can be served by searching the above information:
3.1 English word.
3.2 Pin Yin in English.
3.3 Radical Index of Traditional Chinese Character.

Most fascinatingly, there are incredibly numerous applications from the search results. To list a few:

- Build personal dictionary.
- Build Name List - with Chinese Last Name's sort-key provided, the same Last Name in Chinese will always be grouped together under the sort-key regardless of the different spellings in English.
- Build relational databases such as educational history and relationship data files for the "Parent" in Name List.
- Serve as a great tool for English-Chinese / Chinese-English translation. Again, most fascinatingly, without going to "Chinese School" regularly, it is possible to ubiquitously read the books written in English or Chinese, in addition to learning how to write Traditional Chinese characters efficiently.

Finally, some information regarding the publication: a "pioneer" edition for 百家姓 "The Hundred-Family Surnames" and writings of Radical-Characters was published in March 2022. It will require a set of twelve-part (by Radical Index) to publish the pronunciations and writings for nearly 10,000 Chinese traditional characters and the Part-1 for Stroke No.1 – No.2 was published in July 2022. With all rights reserved, the applications will be available for members only. In addition to English, the data-bases are also designed in preparation of creating the editions of any other languages.

Release September, 2023 or sooner Try For Free

Preface *from the "pioneering" edition*

While I was designing the relational databases for *Ez2Vital Software Inc.*, I came up with the "algorithm" for building the Last Name as part of a key – by using the "Radical Index" vastly used in Chinese dictionaries (there were very little variations in different dictionaries regarding the stroke number or sequence). Due to multiple ways of English spellings for pronouncing the same Last Name, it was necessary for me to add some suffixes to make a unique key. For example, my maiden Last Name 鄭, I spell it as **Jeng** since my eldest brother used **Jeng** when he came to the USA to pursue his Ph.D. in the 60s, so our parents and all my siblings used it. However, **Cheng** is commonly used by **Taiwanese** and **Zheng** is usually used by **Chinese**. Therefore, there are three "addresses" for 鄭 in the databases.

This booklet lists the Last Names along with its radical Index and additional strokes. To build unique keys I used sequence found in 百家姓 (the Hundred Family Surnames) as Last Name Indicator. I also include "radical-characters" (Radicals are stand-alone characters) by using Last Name Indicator '000' and additional stroke number '0' as part of the key. The stroke-sequences for writing radical-characters are also included in a separate nineteen-page section with the order of radical stroke number and sequence.

Eventually, the dictionary will be expanded to include as many characters / words as possible. It is designed for writing traditional Chinese characters with correct stroke-sequences (starting with radical-characters) and multiple ways of spelling for pronunciation (starting with Last Names and radical-characters). Again, 鄭 can be found under **C**, **J** and **Z**; all with its unique key. In addition, with the same **sort-key** key, no matter which spelling is used, they will all be grouped under the same **sort-key**. For example, I used **Cheng** as **sort-key** for 鄭, therefore, I will be grouped with other 鄭 s under **C**, neither **J**, nor **Z** – **one place only** when creating a name / class list – without changing my last name to **Cheng** that I never used. I also applied the same idea for a "Plural-Surname" – a Last Name with more than one character. By the same token, with a unique key for each person, it would easily retrieve data by the selection criteria. For example, I will be on TFGH 1967 and NTU 1971 class lists, and NTUC list with my NTU class since the relational databases of my education history contain the information for the selection criteria - with the "parent" record for my name 鄭淑真.

When the software dictionary is ready, I plan to use it for building idioms. For example, 愛人如己 (₄ai ₂ren ₂ru ₃ji) means **Love people as (love) myself** and the meanings for each character can be looked up by using its English spelling for the pronunciation or its radical index information. The software will also serve as an excellent tool by building "personal" dictionaries and only this unprecedented software can sort the same dictionary in different ways for printing the hard copies.

As mentioned in the very beginning, the software was developed for relational databases used in *Ez2Vital Software Inc.*. Therefore, I have no plans to include Simplified Chinese characters.

Finally, many thanks to 洪權 Tim's input of Chinese characters for me to start building the databases and his expertise in EXCEL tremendously helped me with the software design and testing.

鄭淑真

Jane S. J. Lin

October 2020
Pasadena, California, USA

Radical Index
部　首　索　引

【一畫】Stroke No.: 1 Seq.

Radical	Seq.
一	01
丨	02
、	03
丿	04
乙	05
亅	06

【二畫】Stroke No.: 2 Seq.

Radical	Seq.
二	01
亠	02
人(亻)	03
儿	04
入	05
八	06
冂	07
冖	08
冫	09
几	10
凵	11
刀(刂)	12
力	13
勹	14
匕	15
匚	16
匸	17
十	18
卜	19
卩(㔾)	20
厂	21
厶	22
又	23

【三畫】Stroke No.:3 Seq.

Radical	Seq.
口	01
囗	02
土	03
士	04
夂	05
夕	06
大	07
女	08
子	09
宀	10
寸	11
小	12
尢(尣兀)	13
尸	14
屮	15
山	16
巛(川)	17
工	18
己	19
巾	20
干	21
幺	22
广	23
廴	24
廾	25
弋	26
弓	27
彐(彐彑)	28
彡	29
彳	30

【四畫】Stroke No.:4 Seq.

Radical	Seq.
心(忄小)	01
戈	02
戶	03
手	04
支	05
攴(攵)	06
文	07
斗	08
斤	09
方	10
无	11
日	12
曰	13
月	14
木	15
欠	16
止	17
歹	18
殳	19
毋(母)	20
比	21
毛	22
氏	23
气	24
水(氵氺)	25
火(灬)	26
爪(爫)	27
父	28
爻	29
爿	30
片	31
牙	32
牛	33
犬	34

【五畫】Stroke No.:5 Seq.

Radical	Seq.
玄	01
玉(王)	02
瓜	03
瓦	04
甘	05
生	06
用	07
田	08
疋(疋)	09
疒	10
癶	11
白	12
皮	13
皿	14
目(罒)	15
矛	16
矢	17
石	18
示(礻)	19
禸	20
禾	21
穴	22
立	23

【六畫】Stroke No.:6 Seq.

Radical	Seq.
米	01
竹	02
糸	03
缶	04
网(罓罒)	05
羊	06
羽	07
老	08
而	09
耒	10
耳	11
聿	12
肉(月)	13
臣	14
自	15
至	16
臼	17
舌	18
舛	19
舟	20
色	21
艮	22
艸(艹)	23
虍	24
虫	25
血	26
行	27
衣(衤)	28
襾(西)	29

【七畫】Stroke No. 7 Seq.

Radical	Seq.
見	01
角	02
言	03
谷	04
豆	05
豕	06
豸	07
貝	08
赤	09
走	10
足	11
身	12
車	13
辛	14
辰	15
辵(辶)	16
邑(阝) right	17
酉	18
釆	19
里	20

【八畫】Stroke No. 8 Seq.

Radical	Seq.
金	01
長(长)	02
門	03
阜(阝)left	04
隶	05
隹	06
雨	07
青	08
非	09

【九畫】Stroke No. 9 Seq.

Radical	Seq.
面	01
革	02
韋	03
韭	04
音	05
頁	06
風	07
飛	08
食	09
首	10
香	11

【十畫】Stroke No.10 Seq.

Radical	Seq.
馬	01
骨	02
高	03
髟	04
鬥	05
鬯	06
鬲	07
鬼	08

【十一畫】Stroke No.11 Seq.

Radical	Seq.
魚	01
鳥	02
鹵	03
鹿	04
麥	05
麻	06

【十二畫】Stroke No. 12 Seq.

Radical	Seq.
黃	01
黍	02
黑	03
黹	04

【十三畫】Stroke No. 13 Seq.

Radical	Seq.
黽	01
鼎	02
鼓	03
鼠	04

【十四畫】Stroke No. 14 Seq.

Radical	Seq.
鼻	01
齊	02

【十五畫】Stroke No. 15 Seq.

Radical	Seq.
齒	01

【十六畫】Stroke No. 16 Seq.

Radical	Seq.
龍	01
龜	02

【十七畫】Stroke No. 17 Seq.

Radical	Seq.
龠	01

Tone 1 2 3 4
ˉ ／ ˇ ＼

Used in Last Name Sort

<u>Radical Index Stroke: 1</u>

Sequence: 1 — 1 ¹ yi

2 ² yi

3 ⁴ yi

Sequence: 5 乙 ³ yi

<u>Radical Index Stroke: 1</u>

Sequence: 1   —   1 ^{1} yi $\boxed{—}$ $_1$

2 ^{2} yi

3 ^{4} yi

Sequence: 5   乙 ^{3} yi $\boxed{乙}$ $_1$

Radical Index Stroke: 2

Sequence:	1	二	⁴ er	—	二
				1	*2*
Sequence:	3	人	² ren	丿	人
				1	*2*
Sequence:	5	入	⁴ ru	丿	入
				1	*2*
Sequence:	6	八	¹ ba	ノ	八
				1	*2*
Sequence:	12	刀	¹ dao	刁	刀
				1	*2*
Sequence:	13	力	⁴ li	刁	力
				1	*2*
Sequence:	15	匕	³ bi	—	匕
				1	*2*
Sequence:	18	十	² shi	一	十
				1	*2*
Sequence:	19	卜	³ Bu	丨	卜
				1	*2*
Sequence:	21	厂	¹ an	一	厂
				1	*2*
Sequence:	22	厶	¹ si	乙	厶
				1	*2*
Sequence:	23	又	⁴ you	乃	又
				1	*2*

Radical Index Stroke: 3

Sequence:	1	口		³ kou		㇒	冂	口
						1	2	3

Sequence:	3	土		³ tu		一	十	土
						1	2	3

Sequence:	4	士		⁴ shi		一	十	士
						1	2	3

Sequence:	6	夕		⁴ xi		㇒	㇇	夕
						1	2	3

Sequence:	7	大		⁴ da		一	ナ	大
						1	2	3

Sequence:	8	女		³ nu		㇛	乆	女
						1	2	3

Sequence:	9	子	1	³ zi		㇇	了	子
			2	⁰ zi		1	2	3

Sequence:	11	寸		⁴ cun		一	十	寸
						1	2	3

Sequence:	12	小		³ xiao		㇚	㇚	小
						1	2	3

Sequence:	14	尸		¹ shi		㇀	ㄋ	尸
						1	2	3

Sequence:	16	山		¹ Shan		㇑	凵	山
						1	2	3

Sequence:	17	巛		¹ chuan		㇒	川	川
						1	2	3

Sequence:	18	工		¹ gong		一	㇀	工
						1	2	3

Sequence:	19	己		³ ji		㇇	ㄋ	己
						1	2	3

Sequence:	20	巾		¹ jin		㇑	冂	巾
						1	2	3

Sequence:	21	干		¹ Gan		一	二	干
						1	2	3

Sequence:	22	幺		¹ yao		㇒	乡	幺
						1	2	3

Sequence:	23	广		³ yan		丶	一	广
						1	2	3

Sequence:	26	弋		⁴ yi		一	弋	弋
						1	2	3

Sequence:	27	弓		¹ Gong		㇇	ㄋ	弓
						1	2	3

Sequence:	30	彳		⁴ chi		㇒	彳	彳
						1	2	3

Radical Index Stroke: 4

Sequence: 1	心	¹ xin	㇔	心	心	心	
			1	2	3	4	

Sequence: 2	戈	¹ Ge	一	弋	弋	戈	
			1	2	3	4	

Sequence: 3	戶	⁴ Hu	㇒	厂	戶	戶	
			1	2	3	4	

Sequence: 4	手	³ shou	㇒	二	三	手	
			1	2	3	4	

Sequence: 4	才	² Cai	一	十	才		
			1	2	3		

Sequence: 5	支	¹ Zhi	一	十	支	支	
			1	2	3	4	

Sequence: 7	文	² Wen	㇔	亠	𠂊	文	
			1	2	3	4	

Sequence: 8	斗	³ dou	㇔	㇆	三	斗	
			1	2	3	4	

Sequence: 9	斤	¹ jin	㇒	厂	斤	斤	
			1	2	3	4	

Sequence: 10	方	¹ Fang	㇔	亠	方	方	
			1	2	3	4	

Sequence: 11	无	² wu	一	二	𠂇	无	
			1	2	3	4	

Sequence: 12	日	⁴ ri	丨	冂	日	日	
			1	2	3	4	

Sequence: 13	曰	¹ yue	丨	冂	日	曰	
			1	2	3	4	

Sequence: 14	月	⁴ yue	㇒	冂	月	月	
			1	2	3	4	

Sequence: 15	木	⁴ mu	一	十	才	木	
			1	2	3	4	

Sequence: 16	欠	⁴ qian	㇒	𠂊	𠂊	欠	
			1	2	3	4	

Sequence: 17	止	³ zhi	丨	卜	止	止	
			1	2	3	4	

Sequence: 18	歹	³ dai	一	㇇	歹	歹	
			1	2	3	4	

Sequence: 19	殳	¹ Shu	㇒	几	殳	殳	
			1	2	3	4	

Sequence: 20	毋	⁴ wu	𠃋	母	毋	毋	
			1	2	3	4	

Sequence: 20	母	³ Mu	𠃋	母	母	母	母
			1	2	3	4	5

Sequence: 21	比	³ bi	一	匕	比	比	
			1	2	3	4	

Radical Index Stroke: 4

Sequence:	22	毛		² Mao	´	⁼	⁼	毛
					1	2	3	4
Sequence:	23	氏		⁴ shi	´	厂	斤	氏
					1	2	3	4
Sequence:	24	气		⁴ qi	´	厂	乞	气
					1	2	3	4
Sequence:	25	水		³ Shui	亅	刁	水	水
					1	2	3	4
Sequence:	26	火		³ Huo	`	` `	少	火
					1	2	3	4
Sequence:	27	爪		³ zhao	´	厂	爪	爪
					1	2	3	4
Sequence:	28	父		⁴ fu	´	八	父	父
					1	2	3	4
Sequence:	29	爻	1	² yao	´	乂	乄	爻
					1	2	3	4
Sequence:	30	爿	1	² qiang	一	丬	大	爿
					1	2	3	4
			2	⁴ ban				
Sequence:	31	片		⁴ pian	丿	丿	尸	片
					1	2	3	4
Sequence:	32	牙		² Ya	一	匚	牙	牙
					1	2	3	4
Sequence:	33	牛		² Niu	´	乍	二	牛
					1	2	3	4
Sequence:	34	犬		³ quan	一	犬	大	犬
					1	2	3	4

Radical Index Stroke: 5

Sequence:	1	玄	² xuan	`丶`	`一`	`亠`	`玄`	`玄`
Sequence:	2	玉	⁴ yu	`一`	`二`	`干`	`王`	`玉`
Sequence:	2	王	1 ² **Wang**	`一`	`二`	`干`	`王`	
			2 ² **Weng**					
Sequence:	3	瓜	¹ gua	`丿`	`厂`	`爪`	`瓜`	`瓜`
Sequence:	4	瓦	³ wa	`一`	`丆`	`工`	`瓦`	`瓦`
Sequence:	5	甘	¹ **Gan**	`一`	`十`	`廿`	`甘`	`甘`
Sequence:	6	生	¹ sheng	`丿`	`⺧`	`生`	`牛`	`生`
Sequence:	7	用	⁴ yong	`丿`	`冂`	`月`	`月`	`用`
Sequence:	8	田	² **Tian**	`丨`	`冂`	`日`	`申`	`田`
Sequence:	9	疋	³ pi	`⺕`	`⺶`	`正`	`疋`	`疋`
Sequence:	12	白	² **Bai**	`丿`	`亻`	`白`	`白`	`白`
Sequence:	13	皮	² **Pi**	`丿`	`厂`	`广`	`皮`	`皮`
Sequence:	14	皿	³ min	`丨`	`冂`	`皿`	`皿`	`皿`
Sequence:	15	目	⁴ mu	`丨`	`冂`	`目`	`目`	`目`
Sequence:	16	矛	² mao	`⺇`	`マ`	`予`	`予`	`矛`
Sequence:	17	矢	³ shi	`丿`	`⺅`	`⺥`	`矢`	`矢`
Sequence:	18	石	² **Shi**	`一`	`丆`	`石`	`石`	`石`
Sequence:	19	示	⁴ shi	`一`	`二`	`テ`	`示`	`示`
Sequence:	21	禾	² he	`丿`	`二`	`千`	`禾`	`禾`
Sequence:	22	穴	⁴ xue	`丶`	`⺍`	`⺳`	`穴`	`穴`
Sequence:	23	立	⁴ li	`丶`	`亠`	`⺌`	`立`	`立`

Radical Index Stroke: 6

| Sequence: | 1 | 米 | ³ Mi | ` | `` | 丷 | 半 | 米 | 米 |
| | | | | 1 | 2 | 3 | 4 | 5 | 6 |

| Sequence: | 2 | 竹 | ² Zhu | ノ | ケ | 个 | 你 | 竹 | 竹 |
| | | | | 1 | 2 | 3 | 4 | 5 | 6 |

| Sequence: | 3 | 糸 | ⁴ mi | ` | 幺 | 幺 | 幺 | 糸 | 糸 |
| | | | | 1 | 2 | 3 | 4 | 5 | 6 |

| Sequence: | 4 | 缶 | ³ fou | ノ | ヒ | 乍 | 午 | 缶 | 缶 |
| | | | | 1 | 2 | 3 | 4 | 5 | 6 |

| Sequence: | 5 | 网 | ³ wang | l | 冂 | 冈 | 冈 | 网 | 网 |
| | | | | 1 | 2 | 3 | 4 | 5 | 6 |

| Sequence: | 6 | 羊 | ² yang | ` | 丷 | 兰 | 兰 | 兰 | 羊 |
| | | | | 1 | 2 | 3 | 4 | 5 | 6 |

| Sequence: | 7 | 羽 | ³ yu |] | 习 | 羽 | 羽 | 羽 | 羽 |
| | | | | 1 | 2 | 3 | 4 | 5 | 6 |

| Sequence: | 8 | 老 | ³ lao | 一 | 十 | 土 | 耂 | 耂 | 老 |
| | | | | 1 | 2 | 3 | 4 | 5 | 6 |

| Sequence: | 9 | 而 | ² er | 一 | 丆 | 广 | 而 | 而 | 而 |
| | | | | 1 | 2 | 3 | 4 | 5 | 6 |

| Sequence: | 10 | 耒 | ³ lei | 一 | 二 | 三 | 丰 | 耒 | 耒 |
| | | | | 1 | 2 | 3 | 4 | 5 | 6 |

| Sequence: | 11 | 耳 | ³ er | 一 | 丆 | 丌 | 玌 | 耳 | 耳 |
| | | | | 1 | 2 | 3 | 4 | 5 | 6 |

| Sequence: | 12 | 聿 | ⁴ yu | ⁊ | 彐 | 彐 | 聿 | 聿 | 聿 |
| | | | | 1 | 2 | 3 | 4 | 5 | 6 |

| Sequence: | 13 | 肉 | ⁴ rou | l | 冂 | 内 | 内 | 肉 | 肉 |
| | | | | 1 | 2 | 3 | 4 | 5 | 6 |

| Sequence: | 14 | 臣 | ² chen | 一 | 丆 | 匞 | 臣 | 臣 | 臣 |
| | | | | 1 | 2 | 3 | 4 | 5 | 6 |

| Sequence: | 15 | 自 | ⁴ zi | ' | 亻 | 亻 | 自 | 自 | 自 |
| | | | | 1 | 2 | 3 | 4 | 5 | 6 |

| Sequence: | 16 | 至 | ⁴ zhi | 一 | 工 | 工 | 至 | 至 | 至 |
| | | | | 1 | 2 | 3 | 4 | 5 | 6 |

| Sequence: | 17 | 臼 | ⁴ jiu | ' | 亻 | 亻 | 臼 | 臼 | 臼 |
| | | | | 1 | 2 | 3 | 4 | 5 | 6 |

| Sequence: | 18 | 舌 | ² she | 一 | 二 | 千 | 舌 | 舌 | 舌 |
| | | | | 1 | 2 | 3 | 4 | 5 | 6 |

| Sequence: | 19 | 舛 | ³ chuan | ノ | ク | 夕 | 夕 | 舛 | 舛 |
| | | | | 1 | 2 | 3 | 4 | 5 | 6 |

| Sequence: | 20 | 舟 | ¹ zhou | ' | 亻 | 力 | 舟 | 舟 | 舟 |
| | | | | 1 | 2 | 3 | 4 | 5 | 6 |

| Sequence: | 21 | 色 | ⁴ se | ノ | 夕 | 夕 | 色 | 色 | 色 |
| | | | | 1 | 2 | 3 | 4 | 5 | 6 |

Radical Index Stroke: 6

| Sequence: | 22 | 艮 | 1 | ³ gen | ㄱ | ㅋ | ㅋ | 阝 | 艮 | 艮 |
| | | | 2 | ⁴ gen | 1 | 2 | 3 | 4 | 5 | 6 |

| Sequence: | 23 | 艸 | | ³ cao | ㄴ | ㅂ | 屮 | 屮 | 屮 | 艸 |
| | | | | | 1 | 2 | 3 | 4 | 5 | 6 |

| Sequence: | 25 | 虫 | | ² chong | 丶 | 冂 | 口 | 中 | 虫 | 虫 |
| | | | | | 1 | 2 | 3 | 4 | 5 | 6 |

| Sequence: | 26 | 血 | 1 | ³ xie | 丿 | 亻 | 白 | 血 | 血 | 血 |
| | | | 2 | ² xing | 1 | 2 | 3 | 4 | 5 | 6 |

| Sequence: | 27 | 行 | 1 | ² hang | 丿 | 彳 | 彳 | 彳 | 行 | 行 |
| | | | 2 | ² xing | 1 | 2 | 3 | 4 | 5 | 6 |

| Sequence: | 28 | 衣 | | ¹ Yi | 丶 | 亠 | 广 | 衣 | 衣 | 衣 |
| | | | | | 1 | 2 | 3 | 4 | 5 | 6 |

| Sequence: | 29 | 西 | | ¹ xi | 一 | 厂 | 冂 | 丙 | 西 | 西 |
| | | | | | 1 | 2 | 3 | 4 | 5 | 6 |

Radical Index Stroke: 7

Sequence:	1	見		[4] jian	丨	冂	円	月	目	貝	見
					1	2	3	4	5	6	7
Sequence:	2	角		[3] jiao	⺈	⺈	⼴	角	角	角	角
					1	2	3	4	5	6	7
Sequence:	3	言		[2] Yan	丶	亠	亠	言	言	言	言
					1	2	3	4	5	6	7
Sequence:	4	谷		[3] gu	⼃	八	八	父	谷	谷	谷
					1	2	3	4	5	6	7
Sequence:	5	豆		[4] Dou	一	厂	冃	曰	豆	豆	豆
					1	2	3	4	5	6	7
Sequence:	6	豕		[3] shi	一	豕	丂	豸	豕	豕	豕
					1	2	3	4	5	6	7
Sequence:	7	豸		[4] zhi	⺈	豸	豸	豸	豸	豸	豸
					1	2	3	4	5	6	7
Sequence:	8	貝		[4] Bei	丨	冂	円	月	目	貝	貝
					1	2	3	4	5	6	7
Sequence:	9	赤		[4] chi	一	十	土	赤	赤	赤	赤
					1	2	3	4	5	6	7
Sequence:	10	走		[3] zou	一	十	土	丰	丰	走	走
					1	2	3	4	5	6	7
Sequence:	11	足		[2] zu	丨	冂	口	甼	早	足	足
					1	2	3	4	5	6	7
Sequence:	12	身		[1] shen	⺈	竹	身	身	身	身	身
					1	2	3	4	5	6	7
Sequence:	13	車	1	[1] Che	一	厂	冃	冃	百	亘	車
			2	[1] ju	1	2	3	4	5	6	7
Sequence:	14	辛		[1] Xin	丶	亠	亠	立	立	立	辛
					1	2	3	4	5	6	7
Sequence:	15	辰		[2] chen	一	厂	厂	厈	辰	辰	辰
					1	2	3	4	5	6	7
Sequence:	17	邑		[4] yi	丶	冂	口	吕	吊	吕	邑
					1	2	3	4	5	6	7
Sequence:	18	酉		[3] you	一	厂	冂	丙	西	酉	酉
					1	2	3	4	5	6	7
Sequence:	19	釆		[4] bian	⺈	釆	釆	立	平	釆	釆
					1	2	3	4	5	6	7
Sequence:	20	里		[3] li	丨	冂	日	日	旦	甲	里
					1	2	3	4	5	6	7

Radical Index Stroke: 8

Sequence:	1	金		¹ Jin	丿	入	亼	亽	全	全	余	金
					1	2	3	4	5	6	7	8

Sequence:	2	長	1	² chang	l	匚	F	E	토	툐	長	長
			2	³ zhang	1	2	3	4	5	6	7	8

Sequence:	3	門		² men	丨	冂	冂	門	門	門	門	門
					1	2	3	4	5	6	7	8

Sequence:	4	阜		⁴ fu	′	亻	宀	户	自	自	鸟	阜
					1	2	3	4	5	6	7	8

Sequence:	5	隶	1	⁴ dai	㇇	㇈	㇈	肀	肀	肀	肀	隶
			2	⁴ li	1	2	3	4	5	6	7	8

Sequence:	6	隹		¹ zhui	丿	亻	亻	亻	隹	隹	隹	隹
					1	2	3	4	5	6	7	8

Sequence:	7	雨		³ yu	一	冂	冂	雨	雨	雨	雨	雨
					1	2	3	4	5	6	7	8

Sequence:	8	青	1	¹ ching	一	二	丰	圭	青	青	青	青
			2	¹ qing	1	2	3	4	5	6	7	8

Sequence:	9	非		¹ fei	丿	𠃌	丬	彐	非	非	非	非
					1	2	3	4	5	6	7	8

Radical Index Stroke: 9

Sequence:	1	面	⁴ mian	一	丆	厂	丏	帀	而	而	而	面
				1	2	3	4	5	6	7	8	9
Sequence:	2	革	² ge	一	艹	艹	世	芒	苫	莒	莗	革
				1	2	3	4	5	6	7	8	9
Sequence:	3	韋	² Wei	丆	龶	吉	中	串	韦	韋	韋	韋
				1	2	3	4	5	6	7	8	9
Sequence:	4	韭	³ jiu	丨	丬	丬	丬	韭	非	非	非	韭
				1	2	3	4	5	6	7	8	9
Sequence:	5	音	¹ yin	丶	亠	立	立	立	产	音	音	音
				1	2	3	4	5	6	7	8	9
Sequence:	6	頁	⁴ ye	一	丆	丆	百	百	百	百	頁	頁
				1	2	3	4	5	6	7	8	9
Sequence:	7	風	¹ feng	丿	几	几	凢	凤	凮	風	風	風
				1	2	3	4	5	6	7	8	9
Sequence:	8	飛	¹ fei	乁	乁	飞	飞	飞	飛	飛	飛	飛
				1	2	3	4	5	6	7	8	9
Sequence:	9	食	² shi	丿	人	入	今	今	仐	食	食	食
				1	2	3	4	5	6	7	8	9
Sequence:	10	首	³ shou	丶	丷	丷	丷	产	产	首	首	首
				1	2	3	4	5	6	7	8	9
Sequence:	11	香	¹ xiang	丿	二	千	禾	禾	禾	香	香	香
				1	2	3	4	5	6	7	8	9

Radical Index Stroke: 10

Sequence: 1	馬	³ Ma

丨	厂	𠃌	𠃌	厍	馬	馬	馬	馬
1	2	3	4	5	6	7	8	9

馬
10

Sequence: 2	骨	³ gu

丨	冂	冎	冎	⺆	丹	骨	骨	骨
1	2	3	4	5	6	7	8	9

骨
10

Sequence: 3	高	¹ Gao

丶	亠	亠	六	古	言	高	高	高
1	2	3	4	5	6	7	8	9

高
10

Sequence: 5	鬥	⁴ dou

丨	厂	𠄌	𠄌	𠄌	𠄌	𠄌	𠄌	鬥
1	2	3	4	5	6	7	8	9

鬥
10

Sequence: 6	鬯	⁴ chang

丿	乂	乂	乂	㐅	㳇	幽	幽	幽
1	2	3	4	5	6	7	8	9

鬯
10

Sequence: 7	鬲	² ge

一	冂	冂	鬲	鬲	鬲	鬲	鬲	鬲
1	2	3	4	5	6	7	8	9

鬲
10

Sequence: 8	鬼	³ gui

丿	𠃊	白	白	甶	甶	𠂊	鬼	鬼
1	2	3	4	5	6	7	8	9

鬼
10

Radical Index Stroke: 11

Sequence: 1　魚　² Yu

ノ	ク	ヶ	刍	刍	角	甶	魚	魚
1	2	3	4	5	6	7	8	9

魚	魚
10	11

Sequence: 2　鳥　³ niao

ノ	イ	宀	白	白	自	鳥	鳥	鳥
1	2	3	4	5	6	7	8	9

鳥	鳥
10	11

Sequence: 3　鹵　³ lu

ヽ	ト	广	卣	卤	肉	肉	鹵	鹵
1	2	3	4	5	6	7	8	9

鹵	鹵
10	11

Sequence: 4　鹿　⁴ Lu

ヽ	亠	广	戸	庐	庐	鹿	鹿	鹿
1	2	3	4	5	6	7	8	9

鹿	鹿
10	11

Sequence: 5　麥　⁴ Mai

一	十	圤	굿	夾	夾	夾	夾	夾
1	2	3	4	5	6	7	8	9

麥	麥
10	11

Sequence: 6　麻　² Ma

ヽ	亠	广	广	庁	庁	庥	庥	麻
1	2	3	4	5	6	7	8	9

麻	麻
10	11

Radical Index Stroke: 12

Sequence: 1　黃　² Huang

一	十	卄	廿	芏	丼	芇	苗	苗
1	2	3	4	5	6	7	8	9

昔	黃	黃
10	11	12

Sequence: 2　黍　³ shu

亠	二	千	禾	禾	禾	禾	黍	黍
1	2	3	4	5	6	7	8	9

黍	黍	黍
10	11	12

Sequence: 3　黑　¹ Hei

丶	冂	冂	冂	曰	旦	甲	里	黒
1	2	3	4	5	6	7	8	9

黑	黑	黑
10	11	12

Sequence: 4　黹　³ zhi

丶	丷	丷	丷	业	丱	兴	半	节
1	2	3	4	5	6	7	8	9

黹	黹	黹
10	11	12

Radical Index Stroke: 13

Sequence: 1 黽 ^{3} min

1	2	3	4	5	6	7	8	9

10	11	12	13

Sequence: 2 鼎 ^{3} ding

1	2	3	4	5	6	7	8	9

10	11	12	13

Sequence: 3 鼓 ^{3} gu

1	2	3	4	5	6	7	8	9

10	11	12	13

Sequence: 4 鼠 ^{3} shu

1	2	3	4	5	6	7	8	9

10	11	12	13

Radical Index Stroke: 14

Sequence: 1 鼻 ² bi

´	ͺ	͵	͵	͵	自	自	鼻	鼻
1	2	3	4	5	6	7	8	9

鼻	鼻	鼻	鼻	鼻
10	11	12	13	14

Sequence: 2 齊 ² Qi

`	ͺ	͵	͵	͵	产	产	产	齐
1	2	3	4	5	6	7	8	9

齐	齐	齊	齊	齊
10	11	12	13	14

Radical Index Stroke: 15

Sequence: 1   齒   ³ chi

丨	ㅏ	止	止	屶	屶	歨	岦	峇
1	2	3	4	5	6	7	8	9

齿	齿	齿	齿	齿	齒
10	11	12	13	14	15

Radical Index Stroke: 16

Sequence: 1   龍   ² Long

`	㇇	㇒	㇄	立	产	产	育	育
1	2	3	4	5	6	7	8	9

育	育	龍	龍	龍	龍	龍
10	11	12	13	14	15	16

Sequence: 2   龜   ¹ gui

㇒	㇅	㇇	龟	龟	龟	龟	龟	龟
1	2	3	4	5	6	7	8	9

龜	龜	龜	龜	龜	龜	龜
10	11	12	13	14	15	16

Radical Index Stroke: 17

Sequence: 1   龠   ⁴ yue

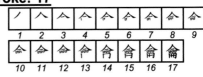

Writing Traditional Chinese Characters
with
Radical Index Stroke No. 1 - No. 2

Radical Index Stroke: 1

Additional Stroke: 0	一	1	[1] yi	一
	一	2	[2] yi	
	一	3	[4] yi	
Additional Stroke: 1	丁		[1] Ding	一 丁
Additional Stroke: 1	七		[1] qi	一 七
Additional Stroke: 2	上	1	[4] shang	丨 卜 上
	上	2	[4] Shang +	
	官		[1] Guan	
Additional Stroke: 2	三		[1] san	一 二 三
Additional Stroke: 2	丈		[4] zhang	一 ナ 丈
Additional Stroke: 2	下		[4] xia	一 丅 下
Additional Stroke: 3	丐		[4] gai	一 丅 干 丐
Additional Stroke: 3	丏		[3] mian	一 丅 丆 丏
Additional Stroke: 3	不		[4] bu	一 ア 不 不
Additional Stroke: 3	丑		[3] chou	乛 刀 丑 丑
Additional Stroke: 4	丘		[1] Qiu	ノ 乍 乍 乕 丘
Additional Stroke: 4	世		[4] shi	一 十 卅 丗 世
Additional Stroke: 4	且		[3] qie	丨 冂 月 月 且
Additional Stroke: 4	丕		[1] pi	一 ア 不 不 丕
Additional Stroke: 4	丙		[3] bing	一 厂 冂 丙 丙
Additional Stroke: 5	丢		[1] diu	一 二 干 壬 丢 丢
Additional Stroke: 5	丞		[2] cheng	乛 了 了 丞 丞 丞
Additional Stroke: 7	並		[4] bing	丶 丷 丷 丷 並 並 並 並

Radical Index Stroke: 1

Sequence: 2 丨

Additional Stroke: 2	丫		*1* ya	`、` `丷` `丫` 1　2
Additional Stroke: 3	中	1	*1* **Zhong**	`丨` `冂` `口` `中` 1　2　3
	中	2	*4* Zhong	
Additional Stroke: 3	丰		*1* feng	`一` `二` `三` `丰` 1　2　3
Additional Stroke: 4	屮		*4* guan	`凵` `屮` `屮` `屮` `屮` 1　2　3　4
Additional Stroke: 6	串		*4* chuan	`丶` `冂` `口` `尸` `呂` `呂` `串` 1　2　3　4　5　6

Sequence: 3 丶

Additional Stroke: 2	凡		*2* **Fan**	`丿` `几` `凡` 1　2
Additional Stroke: 2	丸		*2* wan	`丿` `九` `丸` 1　2
Additional Stroke: 3	丹		*1* dan	`丿` `刀` `丹` `丹` 1　2　3
Additional Stroke: 4	主		*3* zhu	`丶` `亠` `主` `王` `主` 1　2　3　4
Additional Stroke: 5	兵		*1* pang	`一` `厂` `丘` `丘` `丘` `兵` 1　2　3　4　5

Sequence: 4 丿

Additional Stroke: 1	乃		*3* nai	`丿` `乃` 1
Additional Stroke: 1	乂		*4* yi	`丿` `乂` 1
Additional Stroke: 2	久		*3* jiu	`丿` `ク` `久` 1　2
Additional Stroke: 2	么		*1* yao	`丿` `乙` `么` 1　2
Additional Stroke: 3	之		*1* zhi	`丶` `亠` `㇇` `之` 1　2　3
Additional Stroke: 3	尹		*3* yin	`コ` `⺕` `⺕` `尹` 1　2　3
Additional Stroke: 4	乍		*4* zha	`丿` `⺊` `仁` `乍` `乍` 1　2　3　4
Additional Stroke: 4	乎		*1* hu	`一` `丷` `丷` `立` `乎` 1　2　3　4
Additional Stroke: 4	乏		*2* fa	`丿` `丷` `㇈` `乏` `乏` 1　2　3　4

Radical Index Stroke: 1

Sequence: 4 丿

Additional Stroke: 5   乒   ¹ ping

Additional Stroke: 7   乖   ¹ guai

Additional Stroke: 9   乘   ² cheng

Sequence: 5 乙

Additional Stroke: 0   乙   ³ yi

Additional Stroke: 1   乜   ¹ mie

Additional Stroke: 1   九   ³ jiu

Additional Stroke: 2   也   ³ ye

Additional Stroke: 2   乞   ³ qi

Additional Stroke: 5   乩   ¹ ji

Additional Stroke: 7   乳   ³ ru

Additional Stroke: 10   乾 1 ¹ gan

              乾 2 ² qian

Additional Stroke: 12   亂   ⁴ luan

Sequence: 6 亅

Additional Stroke: 1   了 1 ⁰ le

              了 2 ³ liao

Additional Stroke: 3   予 1 ² yu

              予 2 ³ yu

Additional Stroke: 7   事   ⁴ shi

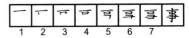

Radical Index Stroke: 2

Sequence: 1 二

Additional Stroke: 0	二		^{4} er
Additional Stroke: 1	于		^{4} chu
Additional Stroke: 1	于		^{2} Yu
Additional Stroke: 2	亓		^{1} Qi
Additional Stroke: 2	井		^{3} Jing
Additional Stroke: 2	五		^{3} Wu
Additional Stroke: 2	云		^{2} yun
Additional Stroke: 2	互		^{4} Hu
Additional Stroke: 4	亙		^{3} gen
Additional Stroke: 6	些		^{1} xie
Additional Stroke: 7	亞		^{3} ya
Additional Stroke: 7	丞	1	^{2} ji
	丞	2	^{4} qi

Radical Index Stroke: 2

Sequence: 2 亠

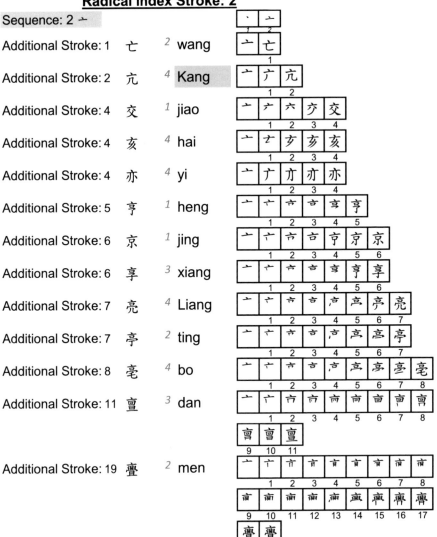

Additional Stroke: 1	亡	2 wang
Additional Stroke: 2	亢	4 Kang
Additional Stroke: 4	交	1 jiao
Additional Stroke: 4	亥	4 hai
Additional Stroke: 4	亦	4 yi
Additional Stroke: 5	亨	1 heng
Additional Stroke: 6	京	1 jing
Additional Stroke: 6	享	3 xiang
Additional Stroke: 7	亮	4 Liang
Additional Stroke: 7	亭	2 ting
Additional Stroke: 8	亳	4 bo
Additional Stroke: 11	亶	3 dan
Additional Stroke: 19	亹	2 men

Radical Index Stroke: 2

Sequence: 3 亻人

ノ 1	亻 2	

Additional Stroke: 0	人		² ren

ノ	人

Additional Stroke: 2	仇		¹ Zhang

亻	𠆢	仇
	1	2

Additional Stroke: 2	仇		² Chou

亻	仂	仇
	1	2

Additional Stroke: 2	仁		¹ Zhang

亻	仁	仁
	1	2

Additional Stroke: 2	化		² Ren

亻	亻-	化
	1	2

Additional Stroke: 2	什	1	² shen

亻	什	什
	1	2

	什	2	² shi

Additional Stroke: 2	仂		⁴ le

亻	仃	仂
	1	2

Additional Stroke: 2	仃		¹ ding

亻	仁	仃
	1	2

Additional Stroke: 2	仆		¹ pu

亻	仈	仆
	1	2

Additional Stroke: 2	仇		² chou

亻	仂	仇
	1	2

Additional Stroke: 2	今		¹ jin

𠆢	𠆢	今
	1	2

Additional Stroke: 2	介		⁴ jie

𠆢	介	介
	1	2

Additional Stroke: 2	仄		⁴ ze

厂	厃	仄
	1	2

Additional Stroke: 2	仍		² reng

亻	仂	仍
	1	2

Additional Stroke: 3	代		⁴ ling

亻	仁	代	代
	1	2	3

Additional Stroke: 3	令	1	⁴ ling

𠆢	𠆢	今	令
	1	2	3

Additional Stroke: 3	令	2	⁴ Ling +

令

	狐		²	hu

狐

Additional Stroke: 3	仝		² Tong

𠆢	𠆢	仝	仝
	1	2	3

Additional Stroke: 3	以		³ yi

丨	丄	𠄌	以
	1	2	3

Additional Stroke: 3	付		⁴ fu

亻	亻-	付	付
	1	2	3

Radical Index Stroke: 2

Sequence: 3 亻人

	丿	亻
	1	2

Additional Stroke: 3　仔　　*3* zi

亻	亻゛	亻了	仔
	1	2	3

Additional Stroke: 3　仕　　*4* shi

亻	仁	仕	仕
	1	2	3

Additional Stroke: 3　他　　*1* ta

亻	亻	仲	他
	1	2	3

Additional Stroke: 3　仗　　*4* zhang

亻	仁	仕	仗
	1	2	3

Additional Stroke: 3　仙　　*1* xian

亻	亻	仙	仙
	1	2	3

Additional Stroke: 3　仞　　*4* ren

亻	亻了	仞	仞
	1	2	3

Additional Stroke: 3　仨　　*1* sa

亻	仁	仨	仨
	1	2	3

Additional Stroke: 4　伊　　*1* Yi

亻	亻゛	伊	伊	伊
	1	2	3	4

Additional Stroke: 4　任　1 *2* Ren

亻	仁	仁	仟	任
	1	2	3	4

　　　　　　　　　　任　2 *4* ren

Additional Stroke: 4　伏　　*2* Fu

亻	仁	仕	伏	伏
	1	2	3	4

Additional Stroke: 4　伍　　*3* Wu

亻	仁	亻了	伍	伍
	1	2	3	4

Additional Stroke: 4　仰　　*3* Yang

亻	亻	化	亻卬	仰
	1	2	3	4

Additional Stroke: 4　仲　1 *4* Zhong

亻	亻	亻口	亻口	仲
	1	2	3	4

　　　　　　　　　　仲　2 *4* Zhong +

　　　　　　　　　　孫　*1* Sun

Additional Stroke: 4　仿　　*3* fan

亻	亻	仁	仿	仿
	1	2	3	4

Additional Stroke: 4　伉　　*4* kang

亻	亻	仁	伉	伉
	1	2	3	4

Additional Stroke: 4　伙　　*3* huo

亻	亻	仪	伙	伙
	1	2	3	4

Additional Stroke: 4　佚　　*1* fu

亻	仁	仁	佚	佚
	1	2	3	4

Radical Index Stroke: 2

Sequence: 3 亻人

	ノ	亻
	1	2

Additional Stroke: 4 伎 ⁴ ji

亻	亻	仁	伎	伎
1	2	3	4	

Additional Stroke: 4 伐 ¹ fa

亻	仁	代	代	伐
1	2	3	4	

Additional Stroke: 4 休 ¹ xiu

亻	仁	什	休	休
1	2	3	4	

Additional Stroke: 4 仵 ³ wu

亻	仁	仁	仁	仵
1	2	3	4	

Additional Stroke: 4 件 ⁴ jian

亻	仁	仁	仁	件
1	2	3	4	

Additional Stroke: 4 仳 ³ pie

亻	仁	仳	仳	仳
1	2	3	4	

Additional Stroke: 4 份 ⁴ fen

亻	仃	份	份	份
1	2	3	4	

Additional Stroke: 4 企 ⁴ qi

𠆢	个	仐	企	企
1	2	3	4	

Additional Stroke: 5 何 1 ² He

何 2 ⁴ he

亻	仁	仁	何	何	何
1	2	3	4	5	

Additional Stroke: 5 余 ² Yu

𠆢	𠆢	合	全	余	余
1	2	3	4	5	

Additional Stroke: 5 佘 ² She

𠆢	𠆢	合	余	佘	佘
1	2	3	4	5	

Additional Stroke: 5 伯 ² Bo

亻	仃	伯	伯	伯	伯
1	2	3	4	5	

Additional Stroke: 5 佟 ² Tong

亻	仁	伫	佟	佟	佟
1	2	3	4	5	

Additional Stroke: 5 佐 ³ Zuo

亻	仁	仁	佐	佐	佐
1	2	3	4	5	

Additional Stroke: 5 住 ⁴ Zhu

亻	仁	仁	仁	住	住
1	2	3	4	5	

Additional Stroke: 5 作 ⁴ zuo

亻	仁	仁	竹	作	作
1	2	3	4	5	

Additional Stroke: 5 位 ⁴ wei

亻	仁	仁	仁	位	位
1	2	3	4	5	

Additional Stroke: 5 佚 ⁴ yi

亻	仁	仁	仁	佚	佚
1	2	3	4	5	

Additional Stroke: 5 佇 ⁴ zhu

亻	仁	仃	仁	佇	佇
1	2	3	4	5	

Additional Stroke: 5 佗 ² tuo

亻	仁	仁	仁	佗	佗
1	2	3	4	5	

Radical Index Stroke: 2

Sequence: 3 亻人

Additional Stroke: 5	佞	[4] ning	
Additional Stroke: 5	伴	[4] ban	
Additional Stroke: 5	佛	[2] fo	
Additional Stroke: 5	估	[1] gu	
Additional Stroke: 5	佑	[4] you	
Additional Stroke: 5	伽 1	[1] jia	
	伽 2	[2] qie	
Additional Stroke: 5	佈	[4] bu	
Additional Stroke: 5	伺 1	[4] ci	
	伺 2	[4] si	
Additional Stroke: 5	伸	[1] shen	
Additional Stroke: 5	佃	[4] dian	
Additional Stroke: 5	佔	[4] zhan	
Additional Stroke: 5	似	[4] si	
Additional Stroke: 5	但	[4] dan	
Additional Stroke: 5	佣	[4] yong	
Additional Stroke: 5	佝	[4] kou	
Additional Stroke: 5	你	[3] ni	
Additional Stroke: 5	低	[1] di	
Additional Stroke: 5	伶	[2] ling	

Radical Index Stroke: 2

				ノ 1	亻 2		

Additional Stroke: 6	俉	² Er	亻 1	仁 2	仁 3	仴 4	俉 5	俉 6	俉

Additional Stroke: 6	來	² Lai	一 1	十 2	十 3	中 4	卆 5	來 6	來

Additional Stroke: 6	佯	² yang	亻 1	仁 2	仁 3	伫 4	佯 5	佯 6	佯

Additional Stroke: 6	依	¹ yi	亻 1	仁 2	仁 3	伊 4	依 5	依 6	依

Additional Stroke: 6	侍	⁴ shi	亻 1	仁 2	仕 3	件 4	侍 5	侍 6	侍

Additional Stroke: 6	佳	¹ jia	亻 1	仁 2	仕 3	住 4	佳 5	佳 6	佳

Additional Stroke: 6	使	³ shi	亻 1	仁 2	仁 3	伃 4	侸 5	使 6	使

Additional Stroke: 6	佬	³ lao	亻 1	仁 2	仕 3	仹 4	伊 5	佬 6	佬

Additional Stroke: 6	供 1	¹ gong	亻 1	仁 2	仕 3	供 4	供 5	供 6	供
	供 2	⁴ gong							

Additional Stroke: 6	例	⁴ li	亻 1	仁 2	仔 3	佡 4	佡 5	例 6	例

Additional Stroke: 6	侃	³ kan	亻 1	仁 2	仢 3	伊 4	伊 5	侃 6	侃

Additional Stroke: 6	佰	³ bai	亻 1	仁 2	仁 3	仔 4	佰 5	佰 6	佰

Additional Stroke: 6	併	⁴ bing	亻 1	仁 2	仁 3	伫 4	伴 5	併 6	併

Additional Stroke: 6	侈	³ chi	亻 1	仁 2	伊 3	伊 4	侈 5	侈 6	侈

Additional Stroke: 6	佩	⁴ pei	亻 1	仈 2	仈 3	佩 4	佩 5	佩 6	佩

Additional Stroke: 6	佻	² tiao	亻 1	仈 2	仈 3	佻 4	佻 5	佻 6	佻

Additional Stroke: 6	侖	² lun	人 1	亼 2	合 3	合 4	侖 5	侖 6	侖

Additional Stroke: 6	份	⁴ yi	亻 1	仁 2	仈 3	价 4	份 5	份 6	份

Additional Stroke: 6	侏	¹ zhu	亻 1	仁 2	仁 3	仁 4	件 5	侏 6	侏

Additional Stroke: 6	佼	³ jiao	亻 1	仁 2	仁 3	仒 4	佽 5	佼 6	佼

Radical Index Stroke: 2

Sequence: 3 亻人

	ノ	亻
		2

Additional Stroke: 6　侗　1　⁴ dong

亻	亻	们	侗	侗	侗	侗
1	2	3	4	5	6	

侗　2　² tong

Additional Stroke: 6　佹　　³ gui

亻	亻	亻	佗	佗	佹	佹
1	2	3	4	5	6	

Additional Stroke: 7　俞　　² Yu

入	亼	介	介	帘	侖	俞	俞
1	2	3	4	5	6	7	

Additional Stroke: 7　侯　1　² Hou

亻	亻	俨	伊	伊	侫	侯	侯
1	2	3	4	5	6	7	

侯　2　⁴ hou

Additional Stroke: 7　保　　³ Bao

亻	亻	侣	伢	但	俘	保	保
1	2	3	4	5	6	7	

Additional Stroke: 7　信　1　⁴ Sing

亻	亻	信	信	信	信	信	信
1	2	3	4	5	6	7	

信　2　⁴ xin

Additional Stroke: 7　俟　　⁴ si

亻	亻	亻	仈	侳	佬	俟	俟
1	2	3	4	5	6	7	

Additional Stroke: 7　俊　　⁴ jun

亻	亻	亻	伀	俗	俊	俊	俊
1	2	3	4	5	6	7	

Additional Stroke: 7　侵　　¹ qin

亻	亻	伊	伊	伊	侵	停	侵
1	2	3	4	5	6	7	

Additional Stroke: 7　便　1　⁴ bian

亻	亻	仁	佰	佰	佰	便	便
1	2	3	4	5	6	7	

便　2　² pian

Additional Stroke: 7　俠　　² xia

亻	亻	仁	仁	佗	佧	俠	俠
1	2	3	4	5	6	7	

Additional Stroke: 7　俑　　³ yong

亻	亻	仔	价	佾	俑	俑	俑
1	2	3	4	5	6	7	

Additional Stroke: 7　俏　　⁴ qiao

亻	亻	亻	仲	伊	俏	俏	俏
1	2	3	4	5	6	7	

Additional Stroke: 7　促　　⁴ cu

亻	亻	俨	伊	伊	俘	促	促
1	2	3	4	5	6	7	

Additional Stroke: 7　侶　　³ lu

亻	亻	伊	伊	伊	俨	侶	侶
1	2	3	4	5	6	7	

Additional Stroke: 7　俘　　² fu

亻	亻	亻	亻	伀	俘	俘	俘
1	2	3	4	5	6	7	

Additional Stroke: 7　俗　　² su

亻	亻	亻	价	俗	俗	俗	俗
1	2	3	4	5	6	7	

Radical Index Stroke: 2

Additional Stroke: 7	俹	³ wu	亻 亻 仁 亿 侉 侉 侉	
Additional Stroke: 7	俐	⁴ li	亻 亻 仨 什 伂 休 伱 俐	
Additional Stroke: 7	俄	⁴ er	亻 亻 仁 什 住 俄 俄 俄	
Additional Stroke: 7	俛	³ mian	亻 亻 仃 伫 侉 侉 侉 俛	
Additional Stroke: 7	係	⁴ xi	亻 亻 仜 伩 係 係 係 係	
Additional Stroke: 7	俚	² li	亻 亻 仃 伊 但 但 俥 俚	
Additional Stroke: 7	俎	³ zu	人 夕 夊 夘 夘 夘 俎 俎	
Additional Stroke: 7	侷	² ju	亻 仃 仃 伊 侷 侷 侷 侷	
Additional Stroke: 8	修	¹ Xiu	亻 亻 亻 仁 伩 佟 修 修
Additional Stroke: 8	倪	² Ni	亻 亻 仁 仨 伵 伵 倪 倪
Additional Stroke: 8	倫	² Lun	亻 亻 价 价 价 侖 倫 倫
Additional Stroke: 8	候	⁴ Hou	亻 亻 仁 仔 伻 侯 侯 候
Additional Stroke: 8	俶 1	⁴ chu	亻 亻 仆 什 什 休 俶 俶
	俶 2	⁴ ti		
Additional Stroke: 8	倓	² tan	亻 亻 仁 伫 伙 伙 倓 倓
Additional Stroke: 8	倌	¹ guan	亻 亻 仁 仁 佗 佗 倌 倌
Additional Stroke: 8	倍	⁴ bei	亻 亻 仁 仁 佋 位 倍 倍
Additional Stroke: 8	俯	³ fu	亻 亻 仁 仨 佇 佭 俯 俯
Additional Stroke: 8	倣	³ fang	亻 亻 仩 伩 伤 份 倣 倣
Additional Stroke: 8	倦	⁴ juan	亻 亻 仁 仁 仨 倖 倦 倦

Radical Index Stroke: 2

Sequence: 3 亻人

ノ	亻

Additional Stroke: 8   控   1   ¹ kong

亻	亻	亻	宀	㣺	㝉	㝏	㝏	控
1	2	3	4	5	6	7	8

　　　　　　　　　　控   2   ³ kong

Additional Stroke: 8   俸   ⁴ feng

亻	仁	仨	仨	伕	侠	俸	俸	俸
1	2	3	4	5	6	7	8

Additional Stroke: 8   倩   ³ qian

亻	仁	仨	仹	佳	佳	倩	倩	倩
1	2	3	4	5	6	7	8

Additional Stroke: 8   倖   ⁴ xing

亻	仁	仁	仕	佳	佳	倖	倖	倖
1	2	3	4	5	6	7	8

Additional Stroke: 8   倆   1   ³ lia

亻	仁	仁	伢	倆	倆	倆	倆	倆
1	2	3	4	5	6	7	8

　　　　　　　　　　倆   2   ³ liang

Additional Stroke: 8   值   ² zhi

亻	仁	仕	估	估	直	值	值	值
1	2	3	4	5	6	7	8

Additional Stroke: 8   借   ⁴ jie

亻	仁	仕	仕	供	供	借	借	借
1	2	3	4	5	6	7	8

Additional Stroke: 8   倚   ³ yi

亻	仁	仕	仧	倚	倚	倚	倚	倚
1	2	3	4	5	6	7	8

Additional Stroke: 8   倒   1   ³ dao

亻	仁	任	任	侄	侄	倒	倒	
1	2	3	4	5	6	7	8

　　　　　　　　　　倒   2   ⁴ dao

Additional Stroke: 8   們   ² men

亻	仈	仲	仲	伊	伊	們	們	們
1	2	3	4	5	6	7	8

Additional Stroke: 8   俺   1   ³ an

亻	仁	伊	伏	伏	俗	俺	俺	
1	2	3	4	5	6	7	8

　　　　　　　　　　俺   2   ⁴ yan

Additional Stroke: 8   倀   ⁴ chang

亻	亻	仁	仼	佴	佴	倀	倀	倀
1	2	3	4	5	6	7	8

Additional Stroke: 8   倔   1   ² jue

亻	仁	仨	伊	伢	倔	倔	倔	倔
1	2	3	4	5	6	7	8

　　　　　　　　　　倔   2   ⁴ jue

Additional Stroke: 8   倨   ⁴ ju

亻	仁	仨	伊	伊	伴	侔	倨	倨
1	2	3	4	5	6	7	8

Additional Stroke: 8   俱   ⁴ ju

亻	仈	们	伯	伯	俱	俱	俱	
1	2	3	4	5	6	7	8

Additional Stroke: 8   倡   ⁴ chang

亻	亻	仴	伊	伊	伊	倡	倡	倡
1	2	3	4	5	6	7	8

Radical Index Stroke: 2

Sequence: 3 亻人

ノ	亻	

Additional Stroke: 8 個 1 *0* ge

亻	们	们	佣	佣	佣	個	個
1	2	3	4	5	6	7	8

個 2 *3* ge

個 3 *4* ge

Additional Stroke: 8 倘 *3* tang

亻	亻	亻	仲	仲	侪	倘	倘
1	2	3	4	5	6	7	8

Additional Stroke: 8 俳 *2* pai

亻	仈	付	身	身	俐	俳	俳
1	2	3	4	5	6	7	8

Additional Stroke: 8 倭 *1* wo

亻	亻	仁	仟	仟	侏	倭	倭
1	2	3	4	5	6	7	8

Additional Stroke: 8 俾 *4* bi

亻	亻	伙	仲	伯	伯	伸	俾
1	2	3	4	5	6	7	8

Additional Stroke: 8 倉 *1* cang

入	亼	今	今	仒	仑	倉	倉
1	2	3	4	5	6	7	8

Additional Stroke: 8 倜 *4* ti

亻	仈	们	佣	佣	佣	倜	倜
1	2	3	4	5	6	7	8

Additional Stroke: 9 偉 *3* wei

亻	仁	仲	俾	仲	俾	偉	偉
1	2	3	4	5	6	7	8

偉
9

Additional Stroke: 9 健 *4* jian

亻	仁	仨	仨	侓	侓	律	健
1	2	3	4	5	6	7	8

健
9

Additional Stroke: 9 偈 1 *4* ji

亻	亻	们	侶	侶	侶	偈	偈
1	2	3	4	5	6	7	8

偈 2 *2* jie

偈
9

Additional Stroke: 9 儹 *2* zan

亻	亻	伊	佟	佟	傚	傚	儹
1	2	3	4	5	6	7	8

儹
9

Additional Stroke: 9 偽 1 *3* wei

亻	亻	仯	伊	偽	偽	偽	偽
1	2	3	4	5	6	7	8

偽 2 *4* wei

偽
9

Additional Stroke: 9 停 *2* ting

亻	亻	广	广	侉	停	停	停
1	2	3	4	5	6	7	8

停
9

Radical Index Stroke: 2

Sequence: 3 亻人

Additional Stroke: 9   假   1   ³ jia

Additional Stroke: 9   偃   ³ yan

Additional Stroke: 9   偌   ⁴ ruo

Additional Stroke: 9   做   ⁴ zuo

Additional Stroke: 9   偶   ³ ou

Additional Stroke: 9   偎   ⁴ wei

Additional Stroke: 9   偕   ² xie

Additional Stroke: 9   偵   ¹ zhen

Additional Stroke: 9   側   ⁴ ce

Additional Stroke: 9   偷   ¹ tou

假   2   ⁴ jia

Radical Index Stroke: 2

Sequence: 3 亻人

ノ	亻
1	2

Additional Stroke: 9　偏　 *1* pian

亻	忄	扩	炉	炉	佭	偏	偏	偏
1	2	3	4	5	6	7	8	

偏
9

Additional Stroke: 9　倏　 *4* shu

亻	亻	忄	竹	攸	攸	倏	倏	倏
1	2	3	4	5	6	7	8	

倏
9

Additional Stroke: 10　傅　 *4* Fu

亻	仁	仃	佰	佰	佰	傅	傅	傅
1	2	3	4	5	6	7	8	

傅	傅
9	10

Additional Stroke: 10　傑　 *2* jie

亻	亻	伋	夕	仈	伮	傑	傑	傑
1	2	3	4	5	6	7	8	

傑	傑
9	10

Additional Stroke: 10　傒　 *1* xi

亻	亻	仾	仾	仾	俓	俓	傒	傒
1	2	3	4	5	6	7	8	

傒	傒
9	10

Additional Stroke: 10　傢　 *1* jia

亻	亻	仾	伫	仾	伫	佲	傢	傢
1	2	3	4	5	6	7	8	

傢	傢
9	10

Additional Stroke: 10　傍　1　 *1* bang

亻	亻	仾	仾	仾	伫	俻	俻	俻
1	2	3	4	5	6	7	8	

傍　2　 *4* bang

俻	傍
9	10

傍　3　 *2* pang

Additional Stroke: 10　傖　 *1* cang

亻	亻	仌	仌	仱	仱	俭	俭	傖
1	2	3	4	5	6	7	8	

傖	傖
9	10

Additional Stroke: 10　備　 *4* bei

亻	仁	仲	伴	供	伊	伊	俻	備
1	2	3	4	5	6	7	8	

備	備
9	10

Additional Stroke: 10　傀　1　 *1* gui

亻	亻	仾	仂	伯	伸	俌	伊	傀
1	2	3	4	5	6	7	8	

傀　2　 *3* kui

傀	傀
9	10

Radical Index Stroke: 2

Sequence: 3 亻人

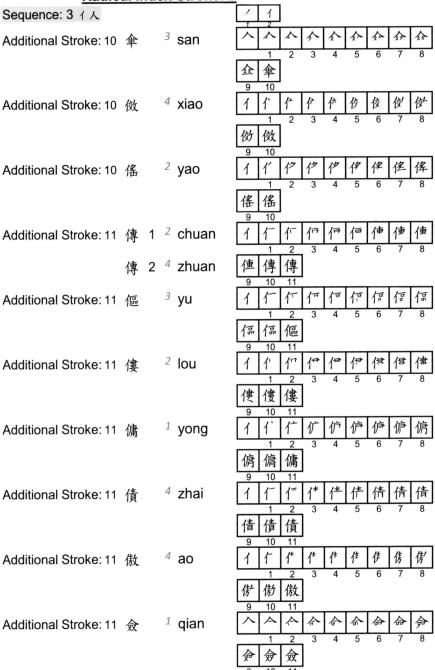

Additional Stroke: 10 傘 ³ san

Additional Stroke: 10 傲 ⁴ xiao

Additional Stroke: 10 傜 ² yao

Additional Stroke: 11 傳 1 ² chuan

傳 2 ⁴ zhuan

Additional Stroke: 11 傴 ³ yu

Additional Stroke: 11 僂 ² lou

Additional Stroke: 11 傭 ¹ yong

Additional Stroke: 11 債 ⁴ zhai

Additional Stroke: 11 傲 ⁴ ao

Additional Stroke: 11 僉 ¹ qian

Radical Index Stroke: 2

ノ	亻

Additional Stroke: 11 僅 *3* jin

Additional Stroke: 11 傾 *1* qing

Additional Stroke: 11 催 *1* cui

Additional Stroke: 11 傷 *1* shang

Additional Stroke: 11 傻 *3* sha

Additional Stroke: 11 傯 *3* zong

Additional Stroke: 12 僧 *1* Seng

Additional Stroke: 12 僮 *2* tong

Additional Stroke: 12 僥 1 *3* jiao

僥 2 *2* yao

Additional Stroke: 12 僖 *1* xi

Radical Index Stroke: 2

Sequence: 3 亻人

ノ	亻
1	2

Additional Stroke: 12 僭   ⁴ jian

亻	亻	仁	伊	俣	僣	僣	僣	僣
1	2	3	4	5	6	7	8	

僣	僣	僣	僭
9	10	11	12

Additional Stroke: 12 僨   ⁴ fen

亻	亻	仆	仕	仕	伴	倍	倩
1	2	3	4	5	6	7	8

僙	債	債	僨
9	10	11	12

Additional Stroke: 12 僚   ² liao

亻	仁	仏	伏	伏	佚	俗	倂
1	2	3	4	5	6	7	8

僗	僚	僚	僚
9	10	11	12

Additional Stroke: 12 焦   ¹ jiao

亻	亻	什	代	伐	作	隹	隹
1	2	3	4	5	6	7	8

隹	焦	焦	焦
9	10	11	12

Additional Stroke: 12 僕   ² pu

亻	亻	亻	仆	仆	伴	伴	僕
1	2	3	4	5	6	7	8

僕	僕	僕	僕
9	10	11	12

Additional Stroke: 12 像   ⁴ xiang

亻	亻	亻	亻	俛	侮	俛	傻
1	2	3	4	5	6	7	8

傻	像	像	像
9	10	11	12

Additional Stroke: 12 僑   ² qiao

亻	亻	仁	伓	伒	侨	倄	侨
1	2	3	4	5	6	7	8

僑	僑	僑	僑
9	10	11	12

Additional Stroke: 12 傕   ⁴ gu

亻	亻	亻	伊	伊	伊	侔	傕
1	2	3	4	5	6	7	8

傕	傕	傕	傕
9	10	11	12

Additional Stroke: 12 棘   ² bo

一	厂	币	市	束	束	束	剌	剌
1	2	3	4	5	6	7	8	9

棘	棘	棘	棘
10	11	12	

Additional Stroke: 13 儀   ² yi

亻	亻	仁	仁	仹	伴	伴	僕
1	2	3	4	5	6	7	8

僕	儀	儀	儀	儀
9	10	11	12	13

Radical Index Stroke: 2

Sequence: 3 亻人

Additional Stroke: 13	儉	³ jian
Additional Stroke: 13	儌	³ jian
Additional Stroke: 13	億	⁴ yi
Additional Stroke: 13	僻	⁴ pi
Additional Stroke: 13	僵	¹ jiang
Additional Stroke: 13	價	⁴ jia
Additional Stroke: 13	儂	² nong
Additional Stroke: 13	儈	⁴ kuai
Additional Stroke: 14	儒	² ru
Additional Stroke: 14	儘	³ jin

Radical Index Stroke: 2

Sequence: 3 亻人

Additional Stroke: 14 儔	² chou
Additional Stroke: 14 儐	¹ bin
Additional Stroke: 14 儕	² chai
Additional Stroke: 15 儲	² Chu
Additional Stroke: 15 優	¹ you
Additional Stroke: 15 償	² chang
Additional Stroke: 15 儡	³ lei
Additional Stroke: 19 儷	⁴ li
Additional Stroke: 20 儼	³ yan

Radical Index Stroke: 2

Sequence: 3 亻人

ノ	亻

Additional Stroke: 20 儻 *3* tang

亻	亻'	亻''	亻'''	亻'''	儻	儻	儻
1	2	3	4	5	6	7	8

儻	儻	儻	儻	儻	儻	儻	儻	儻
9	10	11	12	13	14	15	16	17

儻	儻	儻
18	19	20

Sequence: 4 儿

ノ	儿

Additional Stroke: 2 元 *2* Yuan

一	二	元
1	2	

Additional Stroke: 2 允 *3* yun

ㄥ	ㄆ	允
1	2	

Additional Stroke: 3 充 *1* Chong

一	士	去	充
1	2	3	

Additional Stroke: 3 兄 *1* xiong

丶	冂	口	兄
1	2	3	

Additional Stroke: 4 先 *1* Xian

ノ	㇒	生	生	先
1	2	3	4	

Additional Stroke: 4 光 *1* guang

丨	丬	丷	丄	光
1	2	3	4	

Additional Stroke: 4 兇 *1* xiong

ノ	ㄨ	区	凶	兇
1	2	3	4	

Additional Stroke: 4 兆 *4* zhao

ノ	丿	扌	兆	兆	兆
1	2		3	4	

Additional Stroke: 5 克 *4* ke

一	十	古	古	克	克
1	2	3	4	5	

Additional Stroke: 5 兌 *4* dui

ノ	八	八	兮	台	兌
1	2	3	4	5	

Additional Stroke: 5 免 *3* main

ノ	ㄅ	冃	各	免	免
1	2	3	4	5	

Additional Stroke: 5 兕 *4* si

丨	丨匚	冂	冂	四	兕
1	2	3	4	5	

Additional Stroke: 6 兔 *4* tu

ノ	ㄅ	冃	各	色	免	兔
1	2	3	4	5	6	

Additional Stroke: 6 兒 *2* er

´	亻	乍	臼	臼	臼	兒
1	2	3	4	5	6	

Additional Stroke: 7 兗 *3* yan

丶	二	广	六	产	夻	兗
1	2	3	4	5	6	7

Additional Stroke: 9 兜 *1* dou

´	亻	白	白	自	白	白	白	白
1	2	3	4	5	6	7	8	9

兜

Radical Index Stroke: 2

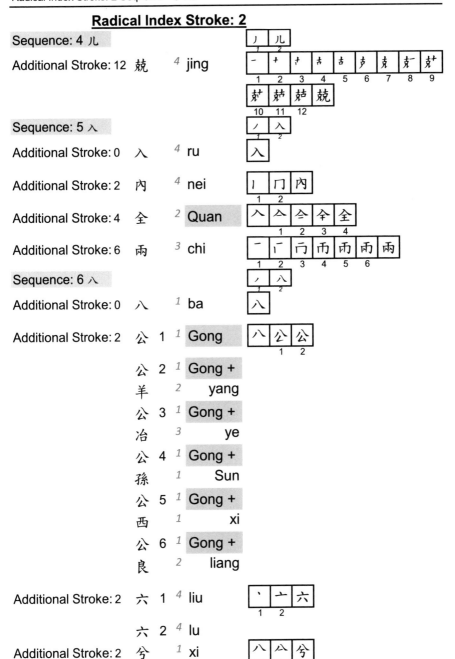

Sequence: 4 儿

Additional Stroke: 12 兢   4 jing

Sequence: 5 入

Additional Stroke: 0 入   4 ru

Additional Stroke: 2 內   4 nei

Additional Stroke: 4 全   2 Quan

Additional Stroke: 6 兩   3 chi

Sequence: 6 八

Additional Stroke: 0 八   1 ba

Additional Stroke: 2 公   1   1 Gong

公   2   1 Gong +

羊   2 yang

公   3   1 Gong +

冶   3 ye

公   4   1 Gong +

孫   1 Sun

公   5   1 Gong +

西   1 xi

公   6   1 Gong +

良   2 liang

Additional Stroke: 2 六   1   4 liu

六   2   4 lu

Additional Stroke: 2 分   1 xi

Radical Index Stroke: 2

Sequence: 6 八

ノ	八
1	2

Additional Stroke: 4   共   ⁴ gong

一	十	艹	共	共
1	2	3	4	

Additional Stroke: 5   兵   ¹ bing

一	丆	丘	斤	丘	兵
1	2	3	4	5	

Additional Stroke: 6   其 1   ² chi

一	十	艹	甘	甘	其	其
1	2	3	4	5	6	

             其 2   ² qi

Additional Stroke: 6   具   ⁴ ju

l	冂	月	月	目	且	具
1	2	3	4	5	6	

Additional Stroke: 6   典   ³ dian

丶	冂	曰	由	曲	典	典
1	2	3	4	5	6	

Additional Stroke: 8   兼   ¹ jian

丶	丷	⺍	彐	半	羊	兼	兼
1	2	3	4	5	6	7	8

Additional Stroke: 14   冀   ⁴ Ji

丶	⺈	刂	北	北	北	背	背	背
1	2	3	4	5	6	7	8	9

背	背	萓	萓	萓	冀
10	11	12	13	14	

Sequence: 7 冂

l	冂
1	2

Additional Stroke: 3   冉   ³ Ran

冂	月	冉	冉
1	2	3	

Additional Stroke: 3   冊   ⁴ ce

冂	川	冊	冊
1	2	3	

Additional Stroke: 4   再   ⁴ zai

一	冂	再	再	再
1	2	3	4	

Additional Stroke: 7   冒   ⁴ mao

冂	冂	曰	冃	冐	冒	冒
1	2	3	4	5	6	7

Additional Stroke: 7   胄   ⁴ zhou

冂	冃	由	由	冑	胄	胄
1	2	3	4	5	6	7

Additional Stroke: 9   冕   ³ mian

冂	冃	曰	罗	罗	罗	罗	罗
1	2	3	4	5	6	7	8

冕
9

Additional Stroke: 10   最   ⁴ zui

冂	冃	曰	且	冐	冐	冐	冐
1	2	3	4	5	6	7	8

最	最
9	10

Radical Index Stroke: 2

Sequence: 8 ⼍

Additional Stroke: 2 冗 *1* guan

Additional Stroke: 7 冠 1 *1* guan

冠 2 *4* guan

Additional Stroke: 8 冤 *1* yuan

Additional Stroke: 8 冥 *2* ming

Additional Stroke: 8 冢 *3* zhong

Additional Stroke: 14 冪 *4* mi

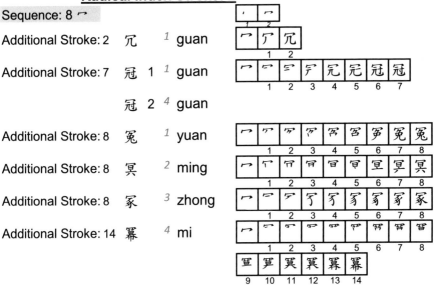

Radical Index Stroke: 2

Sequence: 9 冫

丶	冫
1	2

Additional Stroke: 3　冬　 *1* dong

夂	夂	冬	冬
1	2	3	

Additional Stroke: 4　冰　 *1* bing

冫	冫	冫	冰	冰
1	2	3	4	

Additional Stroke: 5　冷　 *3* Leng

冫	冫	八	伈	冷	冷
1	2	3	4	5	

Additional Stroke: 5　冶　 *3* ye

冫	冫	冫	冶	冶	冶
1	2	3	4	5	

Additional Stroke: 6　洗　 *3* Xian

冫	冫	冫	冼	洗	洗	洗
1	2	3	4	5	6	

Additional Stroke: 6　冽　 *4* lie

冫	冫	冫	歹	歹	冽	冽
1	2	3	4	5	6	

Additional Stroke: 8　凌　 *2* Ling

冫	冫	冫	冫	冫	冫	凌	凌
1	2	3	4	5	6	7	8

Additional Stroke: 8　凍　 *4* dong

冫	冫	冫	沔	沔	沔	沖	凍
1	2	3	4	5	6	7	8

Additional Stroke: 8　准　 *3* zhun

冫	冫	冫	冫	汢	汢	准	准
1	2	3	4	5	6	7	8

Additional Stroke: 8　凋　 *1* diao

冫	冫	刀	汩	汩	汩	凋	凋
1	2	3	4	5	6	7	8

Additional Stroke: 13　凜　 *3* lin

冫	冫	广	广	沪	沪	凉	凉
1	2	3	4	5	6	7	8

澶	澶	凜	凜	凜			
9	10	11	12	13			

Additional Stroke: 14　凝　 *2* ning

冫	冫	斗	斗	斗	斗	斗	凝
1	2	3	4	5	6	7	8

凝	凝	凝	凝	凝	凝		
9	10	11	12	13	14		

Radical Index Stroke: 2

Sequence: 10 几

ノ 1	几 2

Additional Stroke: 0　几　　　*1* ji

几

Additional Stroke: 9　凰　　　*2* huang

几	几	凡	凨	凬	凮	凰	凰
1	2	3	4	5	6	7	8

凰
9

Additional Stroke: 10　凱　　　*3* kai

'	屮	屾	屶	凿	岂	岂	岂	岂
1	2	3	4	5	6	7	8	9

豈	凱
10	

Additional Stroke: 12　凳　　　*4* deng

⁊	⁊	⁊ʹ	⁊ʼ	癶	癶	癶	癶
1	2	3	4	5	6	7	8	9

癶	登	登	凳
10	11	12	

Sequence: 11 凵

ㄴ 1	凵 2

Additional Stroke: 2　凶　　　*1* xiong

ノ	ㄨ	凶
1	2	

Additional Stroke: 3　凹　　　*1* ao

l	ㄈ	𠃊	凹
1	2	3	

Additional Stroke: 3　出　　　*1* chu

l	屮	屮	出
1	2	3	

Additional Stroke: 3　凸　　　*2* tu

'	ㄐ	几	凸
1	2	3	

Additional Stroke: 6　函　　　*2* han

⁊	了	⁊	予	予	承	函
1	2	3	4	5	6	

Radical Index Stroke: 2

Sequence: 12 刀 刂

丶	刂
	2

Additional Stroke: 0   刀   *1* dao

刀

Additional Stroke: 0   刁   *1* Diao

刁

Additional Stroke: 1   刃   *4* ren

刀	刃
	1

Additional Stroke: 2   分   1   *1* fen

丿	八	分
1	2	

              分   2   *4* fen

Additional Stroke: 2   切   1   *1* qie

一	七	切
1	2	

              切   2   *4* qie

Additional Stroke: 2   刈   *4* yi

丿	乂	刈
1	2	

Additional Stroke: 3   刊   *1* kan

一	二	干	刊
1	2	3	

Additional Stroke: 4   列   *4* lie

一	厂	歹	歹	列
1	2	3	4	

Additional Stroke: 4   刑   *2* xing

一	二	干	开	刑
1	2	3	4	

Additional Stroke: 4   刖   *4* yue

丿	几	月	月	刖
1	2	3	4	

Additional Stroke: 4   刎   *3* wen

丿	勹	勺	勿	刎
1	2	3	4	

Additional Stroke: 4   划   *2* hua

一	弋	弋	戈	划
1	2	3	4	

Additional Stroke: 5   别   *2* Bie

丶	冖	口	𠃌	另	别
1	2	3	4	5	

Additional Stroke: 5   利   *4* Li

丿	二	千	禾	禾	利
1	2	3	4	5	

Additional Stroke: 5   初   *1* chu

丶	𬜯	衤	衤	衤	初
1	2	3	4	5	

Additional Stroke: 5   判   *4* pan

	丷	丷	半	半	判
1	2	3	4	5	

Additional Stroke: 5   删   *1* shan

丨	门	刀	𭇛	册	删
1	2	3	4	5	

Additional Stroke: 5   刨   1   *4* bao

丿	勹	勺	包	包	刨
1	2	3	4	5	

              刨   2   *2* pao

Radical Index Stroke: 2

Sequence: 12 刀 刂

丨	刂
	2

Additional Stroke: 6	刻	1	[1] ke

丶	亠	圡	歺	亥	亥	刻
1	2	3	4	5	6	

	刻	2	[4] ke

Additional Stroke: 6	券	[4] quan

丶	丷	丷	亼	半	关	券
1	2	3	4	5	6	

Additional Stroke: 6	刷	[1] shua

丿	尸	尸	尸	吊	吊	刷
1	2	3	4	5	6	

Additional Stroke: 6	刺	[4] ci

一	冖	市	市	束	束	刺
1	2	3	4	5	6	

Additional Stroke: 6	到	[4] dao

一	工	五	至	至	至	到
1	2	3	4	5	6	

Additional Stroke: 6	刮	[1] gua

丿	二	千	舌	舌	舌	刮
1	2	3	4	5	6	

Additional Stroke: 6	制	[4] zhi

丿	广	仁	乍	告	制	制
1	2	3	4	5	6	

Additional Stroke: 6	剁	[4] duo

丿	几	凡	朵	朵	朵	剁
1	2	3	4	5	6	

Additional Stroke: 7	剎	[4] cha

丿	乂	羊	羊	杀	杀	杀	剎
1	2	3	4	5	6	7	

Additional Stroke: 7	剃	[4] ti

丶	丷	半	峃	峃	弟	弟	剃
1	2	3	4	5	6	7	

Additional Stroke: 7	剉	[4] cuo

丿	人	亻	从	丛	坐	坐	剉
1	2	3	4	5	6	7	

Additional Stroke: 7	剄	[3] jing

一	乛	巠	巠	巠	巠	巠	剄
1	2	3	4	5	6	7	

Additional Stroke: 7	削	1	[1] xiao

丨	丬	业	广	肖	肖	肖	削
1	2	3	4	5	6	7	

	削	2	[4] xue

Additional Stroke: 7	前	[2] qian

丶	丷	兰	产	屰	前	前	前
1	2	3	4	5	6	7	

Additional Stroke: 7	剌	[4] la

一	乛	冂	曰	束	束	束	剌
1	2	3	4	5	6	7	

Additional Stroke: 7	剋	[4] ke

一	十	士	古	古	声	克	剋
1	2	3	4	5	6	7	

Additional Stroke: 7	則	[2] ze

丨	冂	冂	月	目	貝	貝	則
1	2	3	4	5	6	7	

Additional Stroke: 8	剛	[1] Gang

丨	冂	冂	冋	冈	冈	岡	岡	剛
1	2	3	4	5	6	7	8	

Radical Index Stroke: 2

Sequence: 12 刀 刂

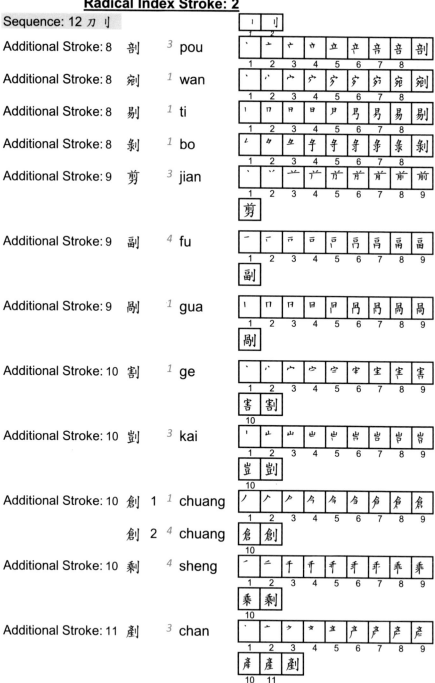

Additional Stroke: 8	剖	*3* pou
Additional Stroke: 8	剜	*1* wan
Additional Stroke: 8	剔	*1* ti
Additional Stroke: 8	剝	*1* bo
Additional Stroke: 9	剪	*3* jian
Additional Stroke: 9	副	*4* fu
Additional Stroke: 9	剮	*1* gua
Additional Stroke: 10	割	*1* ge
Additional Stroke: 10	剴	*3* kai
Additional Stroke: 10	創 1	*1* chuang
	創 2	*4* chuang
Additional Stroke: 10	剩	*4* sheng
Additional Stroke: 11	劇	*3* chan

Radical Index Stroke: 2

Sequence: 12 刀 刂

Additional Stroke: 11 剽 1 [1] biao

剽 2 [2] piao

Additional Stroke: 12 畫 1 [2] hua

劃 2 [4] hua

Additional Stroke: 13 劉 [2] Liu

Additional Stroke: 13 劇 [4] ju

Additional Stroke: 13 劈 [1] pi

Additional Stroke: 13 劍 [4] jan

Additional Stroke: 13 劊 [4] kuai

Additional Stroke: 14 劑 [4] ji

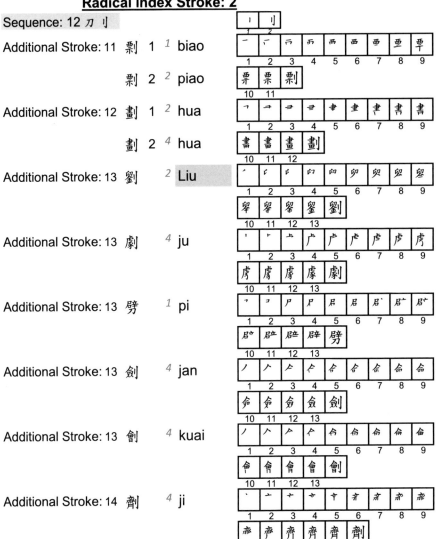

Radical Index Stroke: 2

Sequence: 13 力

			力¹	力²	

Additional Stroke: 0   力   ⁴ li

力

Additional Stroke: 3   加   ¹ jia

力	力	加	加
1	2	3	

Additional Stroke: 3   功   ¹ gong

一	丁	工	功
1	2	3	

Additional Stroke: 4   劣   ² jie

丨	八	小	少	劣
1	2	3	4	

Additional Stroke: 5   劫   ⁴ lie

一	十	土	圭	去	劫
1	2	3	4	5	

Additional Stroke: 5   助   ⁴ zhu

丨	冂	月	月	且	助
1	2	3	4	5	

Additional Stroke: 5   努   ³ nu

乚	女	女	如	奴	努
1	2	3	4	5	

Additional Stroke: 5   劬   ² qu

丿	勹	勹	句	句	劬
1	2	3	4	5	

Additional Stroke: 5   劭   ⁴ shao

乛	刀	刀	召	召	劭
1	2	3	4	5	

Additional Stroke: 6   劾   ² he

丶	亠	亠	歺	亥	亥	劾
1	2	3	4	5	6	

Additional Stroke: 7   勇   ³ yong

乛	乛	厃	甬	甬	甬	甬	勇
1	2	3	4	5	6	7	

Additional Stroke: 7   勉   ³ mian

丿	々	分	备	免	兔	免	勉
1	2	3	4	5	6	7	

Additional Stroke: 7   勃   ² bo

一	十	𠂉	去	㐄	孛	孛	勃
1	2	3	4	5	6	7	

Additional Stroke: 7   勁   ⁴ jing

一	丆	巠	巠	巠	巠	勁
1	2	3	4	5	6	7	

Additional Stroke: 9   勒   ⁴ le

一	十	卄	艹	艹	莒	苩	苩	革
1	2	3	4	5	6	7	8	9

勒

Additional Stroke: 9   務   ⁴ wu

乛	乛	矛	予	矛	矛	矛	務
1	2	3	4	5	6	7	8	9

務

Additional Stroke: 9   勘   ¹ kan

一	十	卄	卄	卄	甚	其	其	甚
1	2	3	4	5	6	7	8	9

勘

Radical Index Stroke: 2

Sequence: 13 力 | コ | 力 |
|---|---|
| 1 | 2 |

Additional Stroke: 9   動   ⁴ dong

ノ	二	仁	后	台	盲	重	重	重
1	2	3	4	5	6	7	8	9

動

Additional Stroke: 9   勖   ⁴ xu

`	冂	冃	日	冃	冐	冐	冐	冒
1	2	3	4	5	6	7	8	9

勖

Additional Stroke: 10   勞   1   ² Lao

勞   2   ⁴ lao

`	` `	ッ	火	火	火`	炒	炏	炏
1	2	3	4	5	6	7	8	9

炏	勞
10	

Additional Stroke: 10   勛   ¹ xun

`	冂	口	尸	号	肙	肙	員	員
1	2	3	4	5	6	7	8	9

員	勛
10	

Additional Stroke: 10   勝   1   ¹ sheng

勝   2   ⁴ sheng

ノ	刀	月	月	月	月`	肝	胖	胖
1	2	3	4	5	6	7	8	9

朕	勝
10	

Additional Stroke: 11   勤   ² qin

一	十	廾	甘	廿	芇	苫	莒	莒
1	2	3	4	5	6	7	8	9

茧	堇	勤
10	11	

Additional Stroke: 11   募   ⁴ mu

`	艹	艹	艹	艹	艹	节	甘	莒
1	2	3	4	5	6	7	8	9

苴	莫	募
10	11	

Additional Stroke: 11   剿   ³ jiao

`	巛	巛	巛	嶋	巤	凿	単	単
1	2	3	4	5	6	7	8	9

巢	巢	剿
10	11	

Additional Stroke: 11   勢   ⁴ shi

一	十	圡	夫	去	坴	坴	刲	執
1	2	3	4	5	6	7	8	9

執	埶	勢
10	11	

Additional Stroke: 14   勳   ¹ xun

ノ	二	仁	后	后	盲	台	重	重
1	2	3	4	5	6	7	8	9

重	重	重	熏	熏	勳
10	11	12	13	14	

Radical Index Stroke: 2

Sequence: 13 力

	ㄱ 力

Additional Stroke: 15 勵 ⁴ li

一	厂	厂	厂	厂	严	严	厉	屚
1	2	3	4	5	6	7	8	9

厝	厝	厲	厲	厲	厲	勵
10	11	12	13	14	15	

Additional Stroke: 18 勸 ⁴ quan

`	⺊	⺊	⺊	⺊	⺊	⺊	芇
1	2	3	4	5	6	7	8	9

茁	芦	苜	苜	莑	萑	萑	雚	雚
10	11	12	13	14	15	16	17	18

勸

Sequence: 14 勹

	ノ 勹

Additional Stroke: 1 勺 1 ² shao

勹	勺
	1

勺 2 ² zhuo

Additional Stroke: 2 勾 ¹ Gou

勹	勼	勾
	1	2

Additional Stroke: 2 勻 ² yun

勹	勺	勻
	1	2

Additional Stroke: 2 勿 ⁴ wu

勹	勿	勿
	1	2

Additional Stroke: 3 包 ¹ Bao

勹	勹	勹	包
	1	2	3

Additional Stroke: 3 匆 ¹ cong

勹	勹	勿	匆
	1	2	3

Additional Stroke: 4 匈 ¹ xiong

勹	勹	勼	匂	匈
	1	2	3	4

Additional Stroke: 7 匍 ² pu

勹	勹	句	句	甫	匍	匍	匍
	1	2	3	4	5	6	7

Additional Stroke: 9 匐 ² fu

勹	勹	句	句	句	句	匐	匐	匐
	1	2	3	4	5	6	7	8

匐
9

Additional Stroke: 9 匏 ² pao

一	ナ	大	太	夸	夸	匏	匏	匏
1	2	3	4	5	6		7	8

匏
9

Radical Index Stroke: 2

Sequence: 15 匕

Additional Stroke: 0   匕   ³ bi

Additional Stroke: 2   化   ⁴ hua

Additional Stroke: 3   北   1 ³ bei

北   2 ⁴ bei

Additional Stroke: 9   匙   1 ² chi

匙   2 ³ shi

Sequence: 16 匚

Additional Stroke: 3   匝   ¹ za

Additional Stroke: 4   匡   ¹ Quang

Additional Stroke: 4   匠   ⁴ jiang

Additional Stroke: 5   匣   ² xia

Additional Stroke: 8   匪   ³ fei

Additional Stroke: 11   匯   ⁴ hui

Additional Stroke: 12   匱   ⁴ kui

Radical Index Stroke: 2

Sequence: 17 匚

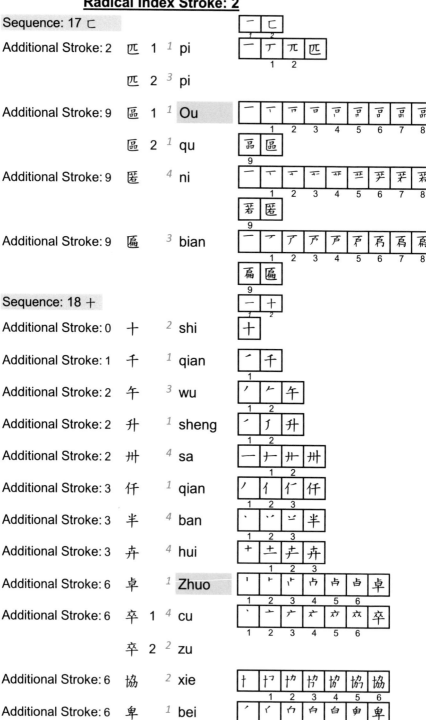

Additional Stroke: 2	匹	1	¹ pi
Additional Stroke: 2	匹	2	³ pi
Additional Stroke: 9	區	1	¹ Ou
Additional Stroke: 9	區	2	¹ qu
Additional Stroke: 9	匿		⁴ ni
Additional Stroke: 9	匾		³ bian

Sequence: 18 十

Additional Stroke: 0	十		² shi
Additional Stroke: 1	千		¹ qian
Additional Stroke: 2	午		³ wu
Additional Stroke: 2	升		¹ sheng
Additional Stroke: 2	卅		⁴ sa
Additional Stroke: 3	仟		¹ qian
Additional Stroke: 3	半		⁴ ban
Additional Stroke: 3	卉		⁴ hui
Additional Stroke: 6	卓		¹ Zhuo
Additional Stroke: 6	卒	1	⁴ cu
Additional Stroke: 6	卒	2	² zu
Additional Stroke: 6	協		² xie
Additional Stroke: 6	卑		¹ bei

Radical Index Stroke: 2

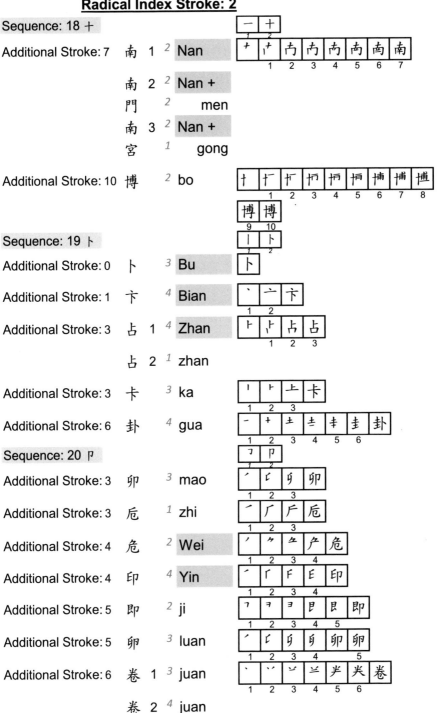

Sequence: 18 十

Additional Stroke: 7   南   1   ² Nan

南   2   ² Nan +
門   ²   men
南   3   ² Nan +
宮   ¹   gong

Additional Stroke: 10   博   ² bo

Sequence: 19 卜

Additional Stroke: 0   卜   ³ Bu

Additional Stroke: 1   卞   ⁴ Bian

Additional Stroke: 3   占   1   ⁴ Zhan

占   2   ¹ zhan

Additional Stroke: 3   卡   ³ ka

Additional Stroke: 6   卦   ⁴ gua

Sequence: 20 卩

Additional Stroke: 3   卯   ³ mao

Additional Stroke: 3   厄   ¹ zhi

Additional Stroke: 4   危   ² Wei

Additional Stroke: 4   印   ⁴ Yin

Additional Stroke: 5   即   ² ji

Additional Stroke: 5   卵   ³ luan

Additional Stroke: 6   卷   1   ³ juan

卷   2   ⁴ juan

Radical Index Stroke: 2

Sequence: 20 卩

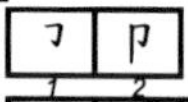

Additional Stroke: 6 卸 4 xie

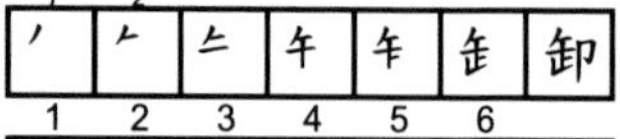

Additional Stroke: 6 卹 4 xu

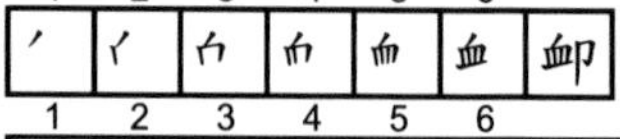

Additional Stroke: 7 郤 4 Que

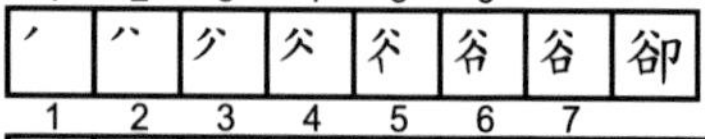

Additional Stroke: 8 卿 1 Qing

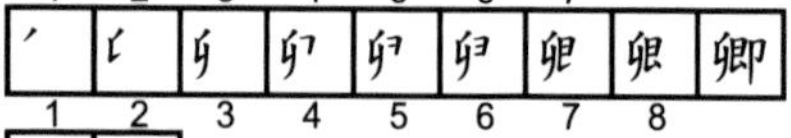

Sequence: 21 厂

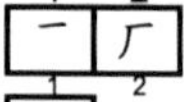

Additional Stroke: 0 厂 1 an

Additional Stroke: 2 厄 4 er

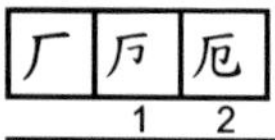

Additional Stroke: 7 厙 4 She

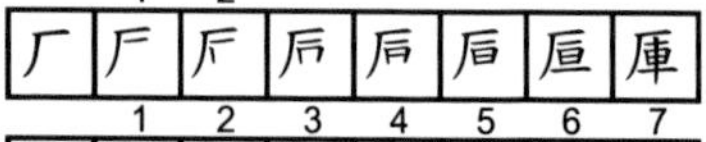

Additional Stroke: 7 厚 4 Hou

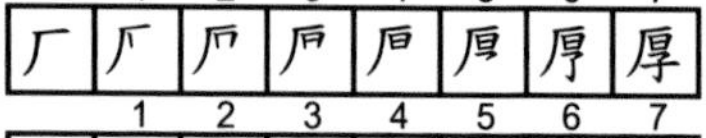

Additional Stroke: 7 厘 2 li

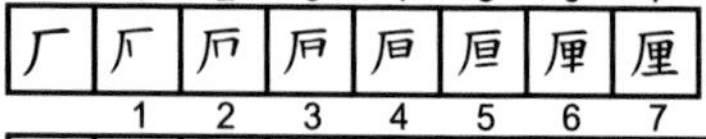

Additional Stroke: 8 原 2 Yuan

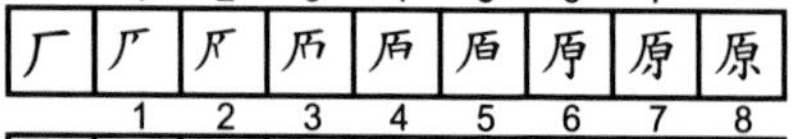

Additional Stroke: 8 厝 4 cuo

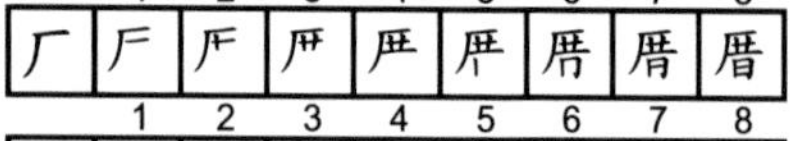

Additional Stroke: 10 厥 2 jue

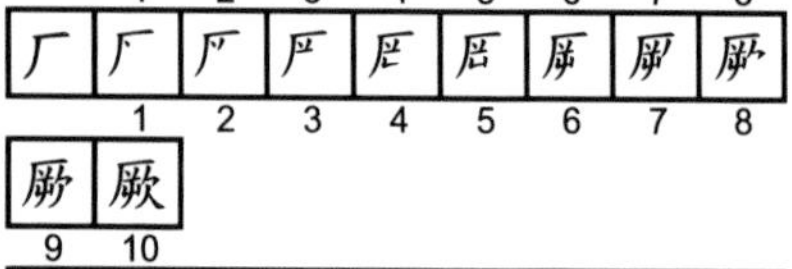

Additional Stroke: 12 厭 4 yan

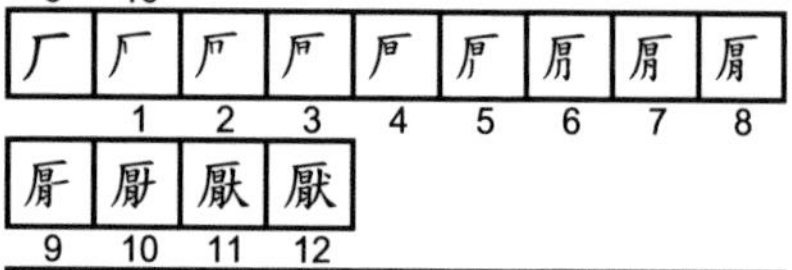

Additional Stroke: 13 厲 4 Li

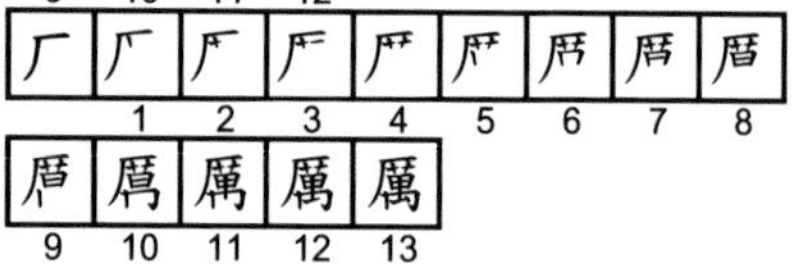

Radical Index Stroke: 2

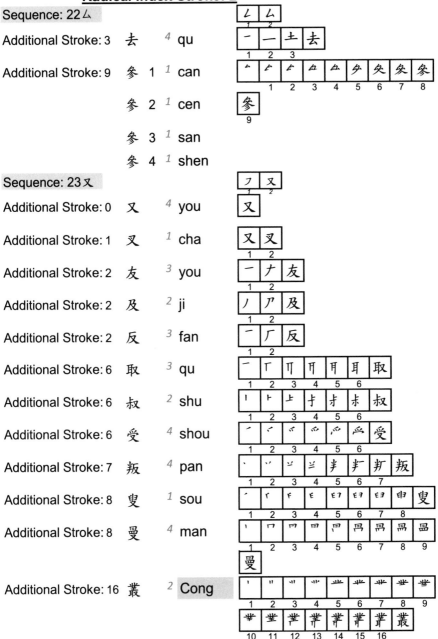

Sequence: 22 ㄥ

Additional Stroke: 3　去　　⁴ qu

Additional Stroke: 9　參　1　¹ can

　　　　　　　　　參　2　¹ cen

　　　　　　　　　參　3　¹ san

　　　　　　　　　參　4　¹ shen

Sequence: 23 又

Additional Stroke: 0　又　　⁴ you

Additional Stroke: 1　叉　　¹ cha

Additional Stroke: 2　友　　³ you

Additional Stroke: 2　及　　² ji

Additional Stroke: 2　反　　³ fan

Additional Stroke: 6　取　　³ qu

Additional Stroke: 6　叔　　² shu

Additional Stroke: 6　受　　⁴ shou

Additional Stroke: 7　叛　　⁴ pan

Additional Stroke: 8　叟　　¹ sou

Additional Stroke: 8　曼　　⁴ man

Additional Stroke: 16　叢　　² Cong

Pronunciation (spelled in English) of Traditional Chinese Characters
with
Radical Index Stroke No. 1 - No. 2

³ **an** 俺 Radical Stroke: **2** Radical Seq: **3** 亻 Additional Stroke: **8**

⁴ **yan** 俺

¹ **an** 厂 Radical Stroke: **2** Radical Seq: **21** 厂 Additional Stroke: **0**

⁴ **ao** 傲 Radical Stroke: **2** Radical Seq: **3** 亻 Additional Stroke: **11**

¹ **ao** 凹 Radical Stroke: **2** Radical Seq: **11** 凵 Additional Stroke: **3**

B								B
3	bai	佰	Radical Stroke: **2**	Radical Seq: **3**	亻	Additional Stroke: **6**	
4	ban	伴	Radical Stroke: **2**	Radical Seq: **3**	亻	Additional Stroke: **5**	
4	ban	半	Radical Stroke: **2**	Radical Seq: **18**	十	Additional Stroke: **3**	
1	bang	傍	Radical Stroke: **2**	Radical Seq: **3**	亻	Additional Stroke: **10**	
4	bang	傍					
2	pang	傍					
3	**Bao**	保	Radical Stroke: **2**	Radical Seq: **3**	亻	Additional Stroke: **7**	
1	**Ba**	八	Radical Stroke: **2**	Radical Seq: **6**	八	Additional Stroke: **0**	
4	bao	刨	Radical Stroke: **2**	Radical Seq: **12**	刂	Additional Stroke: **5**	
2	pao	刨					
1	**Bao**	包	Radical Stroke: **2**	Radical Seq: **14**	勹	Additional Stroke: **3**	
4	bei	倍	Radical Stroke: **2**	Radical Seq: **3**	亻	Additional Stroke: **8**	
4	bei	備	Radical Stroke: **2**	Radical Seq: **3**	亻	Additional Stroke: **10**	
3	bei	北	Radical Stroke: **2**	Radical Seq: **15**	匕	Additional Stroke: **3**	
4	bei	北					
1	bei	卑	Radical Stroke: **2**	Radical Seq: **18**	十	Additional Stroke: **6**	
4	bi	俾	Radical Stroke: **2**	Radical Seq: **3**	亻	Additional Stroke: **8**	

B   **B**

			Radical	Radical		Additional
3	**bi**	匕	Stroke: **2**	Seq: **15**	匕	Stroke: **0**
4	**bian**	便	Stroke: **2**	Seq: **3**	亻	Stroke: **7**
2	**pian**	便				
3	**bian**	區	Stroke: **2**	Seq: **17**	匚	Stroke: **9**
4	**Bian**	卞	Stroke: **2**	Seq: **19**	卜	Stroke: **2**
1	**biao**	剽	Stroke: **2**	Seq: **12**	刂	Stroke: **11**
2	**piao**	剽				
2	**Bie**	別	Stroke: **2**	Seq: **12**	刂	Stroke: **5**
1	**bin**	儐	Stroke: **2**	Seq: **3**	亻	Stroke: **14**
3	**bing**	丙	Stroke: **1**	Seq: **1**	一	Stroke: **4**
4	**bing**	並	Stroke: **1**	Seq: **1**	一	Stroke: **7**
4	**bing**	併	Stroke: **2**	Seq: **3**	亻	Stroke: **6**
1	**bing**	兵	Stroke: **2**	Seq: **6**	八	Stroke: **5**
1	**bing**	冰	Stroke: **2**	Seq: **9**	冫	Stroke: **4**
4	**bo**	亳	Stroke: **2**	Seq: **2**	亠	Stroke: **8**
2	**Bo**	伯	Stroke: **2**	Seq: **3**	亻	Stroke: **5**
2	**bo**	僰	Stroke: **2**	Seq: **3**	人	Stroke: **12**

B

1 **bo**	剝	Radical Stroke: **2**	Radical Seq: **12**	刂	Additional Stroke: **8**	B
2 **bo**	勃	Radical Stroke: **2**	Radical Seq: **13**	力	Additional Stroke: **7**	
2 **bo**	博	Radical Stroke: **2**	Radical Seq: **18**	十	Additional Stroke: **10**	
4 **bu**	不	Radical Stroke: **1**	Radical Seq: **1**	一	Additional Stroke: **3**	
4 **bu**	佈	Radical Stroke: **2**	Radical Seq: **3**	亻	Additional Stroke: **5**	
3 **Bu**	卜	Radical Stroke: **2**	Radical Seq: **19**	卜	Additional Stroke: **0**	

C

	Pinyin	Char	Radical Stroke	Radical Seq		Additional Stroke
1	**can**	參	2	22	ㄙ	9
1	**cen**	參				
1	**san**	參				
1	**shen**	參				
1	**cang**	倉	2	3	人	8
1	**cang**	傖	2	3	亻	10
4	**ce**	側	2	3	亻	9
4	**ce**	冊	2	7	冂	3
4	**cha**	剎	2	12	刂	7
1	**cha**	叉	2	23	又	1
2	**chai**	儕	2	3	亻	14
3	**chan**	劖	2	12	刂	11
1	**chang**	倀	2	3	亻	8
4	**chang**	倡	2	3	亻	8
2	**chang**	償	2	3	亻	15
2	**cheng**	丞	1	1	一	5

C

	Pinyin	Char	Radical Stroke	Radical Seq	Radical	Additional Stroke
2	cheng	乘	1	4	丿	9
4	sheng	乘				
3	chi	侈	2	3	亻	6
2	chi	其	2	6	八	6
2	qi	其				
2	chi	匙	2	15	匕	9
3	shi	匙				
1	**Chong**	充	2	4	儿	3
2	**Chou**	仇	2	3	亻	2
3	chou	丑	1	1	一	3
2	chou	儔	2	3	亻	14
4	chu	亍	2	1	二	1
4	chu	俶	2	3	亻	8
4	ti	俶				
2	**Chu**	儲	2	3	亻	15
1	chu	出	2	11	凵	3

			Radical Stroke:	Radical Seq:		Additional Stroke:
1	**chu**	初	2	12	刀	5
4	**chuan**	串	1	2	丨	6
2	**chuan**	傳	2	3	亻	11
4	**zhuan**	傳				
1	**chuang**	創	2	12	刂	10
4	**chuang**	創				
4	**ci**	伺	2	3	亻	5
4	**si**	伺				
4	**ci**	刺	2	12	刂	6
1	**cong**	匆	2	14	勹	3
2	**Cong**	叢	2	23	又	16
4	**cu**	促	2	3	亻	7
4	**cu**	卒	2	18	十	6
2	**zu**	卒				
1	**cui**	催	2	3	亻	11
4	**cuo**	剉	2	12	刂	7
4	**cuo**	厝	2	21	厂	8

D

4 **Dai**	代	Radical Stroke: **2**	Radical Seq: **3**	亻	Additional Stroke: **3**
1 **dan**	丹	Radical Stroke: **1**	Radical Seq: **3**	丶	Additional Stroke: **3**
3 **dan**	亶	Radical Stroke: **2**	Radical Seq: **2**	亠	Additional Stroke: **11**
4 **dan**	但	Radical Stroke: **2**	Radical Seq: **3**	亻	Additional Stroke: **5**
3 **dao**	倒	Radical Stroke: **2**	Radical Seq: **3**	亻	Additional Stroke: **8**
4 **dao**	倒				
1 **dao**	刀	Radical Stroke: **2**	Radical Seq: **12**	刀	Additional Stroke: **0**
4 **dao**	到	Radical Stroke: **2**	Radical Seq: **12**	刂	Additional Stroke: **6**
4 **deng**	凳	Radical Stroke: **2**	Radical Seq: **10**	几	Additional Stroke: **12**
1 **di**	低	Radical Stroke: **2**	Radical Seq: **3**	亻	Additional Stroke: **5**
4 **dian**	佃	Radical Stroke: **2**	Radical Seq: **3**	亻	Additional Stroke: **5**
3 **dian**	典	Radical Stroke: **2**	Radical Seq: **6**	八	Additional Stroke: **6**
1 **diao**	凋	Radical Stroke: **2**	Radical Seq: **9**	冫	Additional Stroke: **8**
1 **Diao**	刁	Radical Stroke: **2**	Radical Seq: **12**	刀	Additional Stroke: **0**
1 **Ding**	丁	Radical Stroke: **1**	Radical Seq: **1**	一	Additional Stroke: **1**
1 **ding**	仃	Radical Stroke: **2**	Radical Seq: **3**	亻	Additional Stroke: **2**

D

¹ **diu**	丢	Radical Stroke: *1*	Radical Seq: *1*	一	Additional Stroke: *5*
⁴ **dong**	侗	Radical Stroke: *2*	Radical Seq: *3*	亻	Additional Stroke: *6*
² **tong**	侗				
¹ **dong**	冬	Radical Stroke: *2*	Radical Seq: *9*	冫	Additional Stroke: *3*
⁴ **dong**	凍	Radical Stroke: *2*	Radical Seq: *9*	冫	Additional Stroke: *8*
⁴ **dong**	動	Radical Stroke: *2*	Radical Seq: *13*	力	Additional Stroke: *9*
¹ **dou**	兜	Radical Stroke: *2*	Radical Seq: *4*	儿	Additional Stroke: *9*
⁴ **dui**	兌	Radical Stroke: *2*	Radical Seq: *4*	儿	Additional Stroke: *5*
⁴ **duo**	剁	Radical Stroke: *2*	Radical Seq: *12*	刂	Additional Stroke: *6*

D   **D**

_4_ **er**	二	Radical Stroke: **2**	Radical Seq: **1**	二	Additional Stroke: **0**
_2_ **Er**	俚	Radical Stroke: **2**	Radical Seq: **3**	亻	Additional Stroke: **6**
_4_ **er**	俄	Radical Stroke: **2**	Radical Seq: **3**	亻	Additional Stroke: **7**
_2_ **er**	兒	Radical Stroke: **2**	Radical Seq: **4**	儿	Additional Stroke: **6**
_4_ **er**	厄	Radical Stroke: **2**	Radical Seq: **21**	厂	Additional Stroke: **2**

E   E

F

			Radical	Radical		Additional	
2	fa	乏	Stroke: 1	Seq: 4	ノ	Stroke: 4	
1	fa	伐	Stroke: 2	Seq: 3	亻	Stroke: 4	
2	Fan	凡	Stroke: 1	Seq: 3	丶	Stroke: 2	
3	fan	反	Stroke: 2	Seq: 23	又	Stroke: 2	
3	fang	仿	Stroke: 2	Seq: 3	亻	Stroke: 4	
3	fang	傲	Stroke: 2	Seq: 3	亻	Stroke: 8	
3	fei	匪	Stroke: 2	Seq: 16	匚	Stroke: 8	
4	fen	份	Stroke: 2	Seq: 3	亻	Stroke: 4	
4	fen	僨	Stroke: 2	Seq: 3	亻	Stroke: 12	
1	fen	分	Stroke: 2	Seq: 12	刀	Stroke: 2	
4	fen	分					
1	feng	丰	Stroke: 1	Seq: 2	丨	Stroke: 3	
4	feng	俸	Stroke: 2	Seq: 3	亻	Stroke: 8	
2	fo	佛	Stroke: 2	Seq: 3	亻	Stroke: 5	
4	fu	付	Stroke: 2	Seq: 3	亻	Stroke: 3	
2	Fu	伏	Stroke: 2	Seq: 3	亻	Stroke: 4	

F

			Radical	Radical		Additional
1	**fu**	佚	Stroke: **2**	Seq: **3**	亻	Stroke: **4**
2	**fu**	俘	Stroke: **2**	Seq: **3**	亻	Stroke: **7**
3	**fu**	俯	Stroke: **2**	Seq: **3**	亻	Stroke: **8**
4	**Fu**	傅	Stroke: **2**	Seq: **3**	亻	Stroke: **10**
4	**fu**	副	Stroke: **2**	Seq: **12**	刂	Stroke: **9**
2	**fu**	匍	Stroke: **2**	Seq: **14**	勹	Stroke: **9**

F

F

4 gai	丐	Radical Stroke: **1**	Radical Seq: **1**	一	Additional Stroke: **3**	
1 gan	乾	Radical Stroke: **1**	Radical Seq: **5**	乙	Additional Stroke: **10**	
2 qian	乾					
1 **Gang**	剛	Radical Stroke: **2**	Radical Seq: **12**	刂	Additional Stroke: **8**	
0 ge	個	Radical Stroke: **2**	Radical Seq: **3**	亻	Additional Stroke: **8**	
3 ge						
4 ge						
1 ge	割	Radical Stroke: **2**	Radical Seq: **12**	刂	Additional Stroke: **10**	
3 gen	亙	Radical Stroke: **2**	Radical Seq: **1**	二	Additional Stroke: **4**	
1 gong	供	Radical Stroke: **2**	Radical Seq: **3**	亻	Additional Stroke: **6**	
4 gong	供					
1 **Gong**	公	Radical Stroke: **2**	Radical Seq: **6**	八	Additional Stroke: **2**	
1 **Gong +**	公	Radical Stroke: **2**	Radical Seq: **6**	八	Additional Stroke: **2**	
2 yang	羊	Radical Stroke: **6**	Radical Seq: **6**	羊	Additional Stroke: **0**	
1 **Gong +**	公	Radical Stroke: **2**	Radical Seq: **6**	八	Additional Stroke: **2**	
3 ye	冶	Radical Stroke: **2**	Radical Seq: **9**	冫	Additional Stroke: **5**	

G   G

			Radical Stroke: 2	Radical Seq: 6	八	Additional Stroke: 2
1	**Gong +**	公	Radical Stroke: 2	Radical Seq: 6	八	Additional Stroke: 2
1	**sun**	孫	Radical Stroke: 3	Radical Seq: 9	子	Additional Stroke: 7
1	**Gong +**	公	Radical Stroke: 2	Radical Seq: 6	八	Additional Stroke: 2
1	**xi**	西	Radical Stroke: 6	Radical Seq: 29	西	Additional Stroke: 1
1	**Gong +**	公	Radical Stroke: 2	Radical Seq: 6	八	Additional Stroke: 2
2	**Liang**	良	Radical Stroke: 6	Radical Seq: 22	艮	Additional Stroke: 1
4	**gong**	共	Radical Stroke: 2	Radical Seq: 6	八	Additional Stroke: 4
1	**gong**	功	Radical Stroke: 2	Radical Seq: 13	力	Additional Stroke: 3
1	**Gou**	勾	Radical Stroke: 2	Radical Seq: 14	勹	Additional Stroke: 2
1	**gu**	估	Radical Stroke: 2	Radical Seq: 3	亻	Additional Stroke: 5
4	**gu**	僱	Radical Stroke: 2	Radical Seq: 3	亻	Additional Stroke: 12
1	**gua**	刮	Radical Stroke: 2	Radical Seq: 12	刂	Additional Stroke: 6
3	**gua**	剮	Radical Stroke: 2	Radical Seq: 12	刂	Additional Stroke: 9
4	**gua**	卦	Radical Stroke: 2	Radical Seq: 19	卜	Additional Stroke: 6
1	**guai**	乖	Radical Stroke: 1	Radical Seq: 4	丿	Additional Stroke: 7
4	**guan**	丱	Radical Stroke: 1	Radical Seq: 2	丨	Additional Stroke: 4

G   G

1 **guan**	倌	Radical Stroke: **2**	Radical Seq: **3**	亻	Additional Stroke: **8**
1 **guan**	冠	Radical Stroke: **2**	Radical Seq: **8**	冖	Additional Stroke: **7**
4 **guan**	冠				
1 **guang**	光	Radical Stroke: **2**	Radical Seq: **4**	儿	Additional Stroke: **4**
3 **gui**	佹	Radical Stroke: **2**	Radical Seq: **3**	亻	Additional Stroke: **6**
1 **gui**	傀	Radical Stroke: **2**	Radical Seq: **3**	亻	Additional Stroke: **10**
3 **kui**	傀				

G

4	hai	亥	Radical Stroke: ***2***	Radical Seq: ***2***	亠	Additional Stroke: ***4***
2	han	函	Radical Stroke: ***2***	Radical Seq: ***11***	凵	Additional Stroke: ***6***
2	He	何	Radical Stroke: ***2***	Radical Seq: ***3***	亻	Additional Stroke: ***5***
4	he	何				
2	he	劾	Radical Stroke: ***2***	Radical Seq: ***13***	力	Additional Stroke: ***6***
1	heng	亨	Radical Stroke: ***2***	Radical Seq: ***2***	亠	Additional Stroke: ***5***
2	Hou	侯	Radical Stroke: ***2***	Radical Seq: ***3***	亻	Additional Stroke: ***7***
4	hou	侯				
4	Hou	候	Radical Stroke: ***2***	Radical Seq: ***3***	亻	Additional Stroke: ***8***
4	Hou	厚	Radical Stroke: ***2***	Radical Seq: ***21***	厂	Additional Stroke: ***7***
1	hu	乎	Radical Stroke: ***1***	Radical Seq: ***4***	丿	Additional Stroke: ***4***
4	hu	互	Radical Stroke: ***2***	Radical Seq: ***1***	二	Additional Stroke: ***2***
4	Hua	化	Radical Stroke: ***2***	Radical Seq: ***3***	亻	Additional Stroke: ***2***
2	hua	划	Radical Stroke: ***2***	Radical Seq: ***12***	刂	Additional Stroke: ***4***
2	hua	劃	Radical Stroke: ***2***	Radical Seq: ***12***	刂	Additional Stroke: ***12***
4	hua	劃				

4 **hua**	化	Radical Stroke: **2**	Radical Seq: **15**	匕	Additional Stroke: **2**
2 **huang**	凰	Radical Stroke: **2**	Radical Seq: **10**	几	Additional Stroke: **9**
4 **hui**	匯	Radical Stroke: **2**	Radical Seq: **16**	⊏	Additional Stroke: **11**
4 **hui**	卉	Radical Stroke: **2**	Radical Seq: **18**	十	Additional Stroke: **3**
3 **huo**	伙	Radical Stroke: **2**	Radical Seq: **3**	亻	Additional Stroke: **4**

No.	Pinyin	Char	Radical Stroke	Radical Seq	Radical	Additional Stroke
1	ji	乩	1	5	乙	5
2	ji	亟	2	1	二	7
4	qi	亟				
4	ji	伎	2	3	亻	4
4	ji	偈	2	3	亻	9
2	jie	偈				
4	Ji	冀	2	6	八	14
1	ji	几	2	10	几	0
4	ji	劑	2	12	刂	14
2	ji	即	2	20	卩	5
2	ji	及	2	23	又	2
1	jia	伽	2	3	亻	5
2	qie	伽				
1	jia	佳	2	3	亻	6
3	jia	假	2	3	亻	9
4	jia	假				

J

[1] jia	傢	Radical Stroke: **2**	Radical Seq: **3**	亻	Additional Stroke: **10**	
[4] jia	價	Radical Stroke: **2**	Radical Seq: **3**	亻	Additional Stroke: **13**	
[1] jia	加	Radical Stroke: **2**	Radical Seq: **13**	力	Additional Stroke: **3**	
[4] jian	件	Radical Stroke: **2**	Radical Seq: **3**	亻	Additional Stroke: **4**	
[4] jian	健	Radical Stroke: **2**	Radical Seq: **3**	亻	Additional Stroke: **9**	
[4] jian	儹	Radical Stroke: **2**	Radical Seq: **3**	亻	Additional Stroke: **12**	
[3] jian	儉	Radical Stroke: **2**	Radical Seq: **3**	亻	Additional Stroke: **13**	
[1] jian	兼	Radical Stroke: **2**	Radical Seq: **6**	八	Additional Stroke: **8**	
[3] jian	剪	Radical Stroke: **2**	Radical Seq: **12**	刀	Additional Stroke: **9**	
[4] jian	劍	Radical Stroke: **2**	Radical Seq: **12**	刂	Additional Stroke: **13**	
[1] jiang	僵	Radical Stroke: **2**	Radical Seq: **3**	亻	Additional Stroke: **13**	
[4] jiang	匠	Radical Stroke: **2**	Radical Seq: **16**	匚	Additional Stroke: **4**	
[1] jiao	交	Radical Stroke: **2**	Radical Seq: **2**	亠	Additional Stroke: **4**	
[3] jiao	佼	Radical Stroke: **2**	Radical Seq: **3**	亻	Additional Stroke: **6**	
[3] jiao	僥	Radical Stroke: **2**	Radical Seq: **3**	亻	Additional Stroke: **12**	
[2] yao	僥					

J

			Radical	Radical		Additional	
1	jiao	僬	Radical Stroke: **2**	Radical Seq: **3**	亻	Additional Stroke: **12**	
3	jiao	劋	Radical Stroke: **2**	Radical Seq: **12**	刂	Additional Stroke: **11**	
4	jie	介	Radical Stroke: **2**	Radical Seq: **3**	人	Additional Stroke: **2**	
4	jie	借	Radical Stroke: **2**	Radical Seq: **3**	亻	Additional Stroke: **8**	
2	jie	傑	Radical Stroke: **2**	Radical Seq: **3**	亻	Additional Stroke: **10**	
2	jie	劫	Radical Stroke: **2**	Radical Seq: **13**	力	Additional Stroke: **5**	
1	jin	今	Radical Stroke: **2**	Radical Seq: **3**	人	Additional Stroke: **2**	
3	jin	僅	Radical Stroke: **2**	Radical Seq: **3**	亻	Additional Stroke: **11**	
3	jin	儘	Radical Stroke: **2**	Radical Seq: **3**	亻	Additional Stroke: **14**	
3	Jing	井	Radical Stroke: **2**	Radical Seq: **1**	二	Additional Stroke: **2**	
1	jing	京	Radical Stroke: **2**	Radical Seq: **2**	亠	Additional Stroke: **6**	
3	jing	儆	Radical Stroke: **2**	Radical Seq: **3**	亻	Additional Stroke: **13**	
4	jing	兢	Radical Stroke: **2**	Radical Seq: **4**	儿	Additional Stroke: **12**	
3	jing	剄	Radical Stroke: **2**	Radical Seq: **12**	刂	Additional Stroke: **7**	
4	jing	勁	Radical Stroke: **2**	Radical Seq: **13**	力	Additional Stroke: **7**	
3	jiu	久	Radical Stroke: **1**	Radical Seq: **4**	丿	Additional Stroke: **2**	

J   J

3 **jiu**	九	Radical Stroke: **1**	Radical Seq: **5**	乙	Additional Stroke: **1**
2 **ju**	侷	Radical Stroke: **2**	Radical Seq: **3**	亻	Additional Stroke: **7**
4 **ju**	倨	Radical Stroke: **2**	Radical Seq: **3**	亻	Additional Stroke: **8**
4 **ju**	俱	Radical Stroke: **2**	Radical Seq: **3**	亻	Additional Stroke: **8**
4 **ju**	具	Radical Stroke: **2**	Radical Seq: **6**	八	Additional Stroke: **6**
4 **ju**	劇	Radical Stroke: **2**	Radical Seq: **12**	刂	Additional Stroke: **13**
4 **juan**	倦	Radical Stroke: **2**	Radical Seq: **3**	亻	Additional Stroke: **8**
3 **juan**	卷	Radical Stroke: **2**	Radical Seq: **20**	卩	Additional Stroke: **6**
4 **juan**	卷				
2 **jue**	倔	Radical Stroke: **2**	Radical Seq: **3**	亻	Additional Stroke: **8**
4 **jue**	倔				
2 **jue**	厥	Radical Stroke: **2**	Radical Seq: **21**	厂	Additional Stroke: **10**
4 **jun**	俊	Radical Stroke: **2**	Radical Seq: **3**	亻	Additional Stroke: **7**

J J

	Pinyin	Char	Radical Stroke	Radical Seq		Additional Stroke
3	ka	卡	2	19	卜	3
3	kai	凱	2	10	几	10
3	kai	剴	2	12	刂	10
3	kan	侃	2	3	亻	6
1	kan	刊	2	12	刂	3
1	kan	勘	2	13	力	9
4	**Kang**	亢	2	2	亠	2
4	kang	伉	2	3	亻	4
4	Ke	克	2	4	儿	5
1	ke	刻	2	12	刂	6
4	ke	刻				
4	ke	剋	2	12	刂	7
1	kong	倥	2	3	亻	8
3	kong	倥				
4	kou	佝	2	3	亻	5
4	kuai	儈	2	3	亻	13

K

_4_ **kuai**	劊	Radical Stroke: **2**	Radical Seq: **12**	刂	Additional Stroke: **13**	
_1_ **Kuang**	匡	Radical Stroke: **2**	Radical Seq: **16**	ㄷ	Additional Stroke: **4**	
_3_ **kui**	傀	Radical Stroke: **2**	Radical Seq: **3**	亻	Additional Stroke: **10**	
_1_ **gui**	傀					
_4_ **kui**	匱	Radical Stroke: **2**	Radical Seq: **16**	ㄷ	Additional Stroke: **12**	

	Pinyin	Char	Radical Stroke	Radical Seq		Additional Stroke
4	la	剌	2	12	刂	7
2	**Lai**	來	2	3	亻	6
3	lao	佬	2	3	亻	6
2	**Lao**	勞	2	13	力	10
4	lao	勞				
0	le	了	1	6	亅	1
3	liao	了				
4	le	仂	2	3	亻	2
4	le	冽	2	9	冫	6
4	le	勒	2	13	力	9
1	lei	儡	2	3	亻	15
3	**Leng**	冷	2	9	冫	5
4	li	例	2	3	亻	6
4	li	俐	2	3	亻	7
2	li	俚	2	3	亻	7
4	li	儷	2	3	亻	19

L

			Radical	Radical		Additional
4	**Li**	利	Stroke: **2**	Seq: **12**	刂	Stroke: **5**
4	li	力	Stroke: **2**	Seq: **13**	力	Stroke: **0**
4	li	勵	Stroke: **2**	Seq: **13**	力	Stroke: **15**
2	li	厘	Stroke: **2**	Seq: **21**	厂	Stroke: **7**
4	**Li**	屬	Stroke: **2**	Seq: **21**	厂	Stroke: **13**
3	lia	倆	Stroke: **2**	Seq: **3**	亻	Stroke: **8**
3	liang					
4	liang	亮	Stroke: **2**	Seq: **2**	亠	Stroke: **7**
3	liang	兩	Stroke: **2**	Seq: **5**	入	Stroke: **6**
2	liao	僚	Stroke: **2**	Seq: **3**	亻	Stroke: **12**
4	lie	列	Stroke: **2**	Seq: **12**	刂	Stroke: **4**
4	lie	劣	Stroke: **2**	Seq: **13**	力	Stroke: **4**
3	lin	凜	Stroke: **2**	Seq: **9**	冫	Stroke: **13**
4	ling	令	Stroke: **2**	Seq: **3**	人	Stroke: **3**
4	**Ling +**	令	Stroke: **2**	Seq: **3**	人	Stroke: **3**
2	hu	狐	Stroke: **4**	Seq: **34**	犬	Stroke: **6**

L   L

2	**ling**	伶	Radical Stroke: **2**	Radical Seq: **3**	亻	Additional Stroke: **5**
2	**Ling**	凌	Radical Stroke: **2**	Radical Seq: **9**	冫	Additional Stroke: **8**
4	**liu**	六	Radical Stroke: **2**	Radical Seq: **6**	八	Additional Stroke: **2**
4	**lu**	六				
2	**Liu**	劉	Radical Stroke: **2**	Radical Seq: **12**	刂	Additional Stroke: **13**
2	**lou**	僂	Radical Stroke: **2**	Radical Seq: **3**	亻	Additional Stroke: **11**
3	**lu**	侶	Radical Stroke: **2**	Radical Seq: **3**	亻	Additional Stroke: **7**
4	**luan**	亂	Radical Stroke: **1**	Radical Seq: **5**	乙	Additional Stroke: **12**
3	**luan**	卵	Radical Stroke: **2**	Radical Seq: **20**	卩	Additional Stroke: **5**
2	**lun**	侖	Radical Stroke: **2**	Radical Seq: **3**	人	Additional Stroke: **6**
2	**Lun**	倫	Radical Stroke: **2**	Radical Seq: **3**	亻	Additional Stroke: **8**

_4_ **man**	曼	Radical Stroke: *2*	Radical Seq: *23*	又	Additional Stroke: *8*	
_4_ **mao**	冒	Radical Stroke: *2*	Radical Seq: *7*	冂	Additional Stroke: *7*	
_3_ **mao**	卯	Radical Stroke: *2*	Radical Seq: *20*	卩	Additional Stroke: *3*	
_2_ **men**	亹	Radical Stroke: *2*	Radical Seq: *2*	亠	Additional Stroke: *19*	
_2_ **men**	們	Radical Stroke: *2*	Radical Seq: *3*	亻	Additional Stroke: *8*	
_4_ **mi**	冪	Radical Stroke: *2*	Radical Seq: *8*	冖	Additional Stroke: *14*	
_3_ **mian**	丏	Radical Stroke: *1*	Radical Seq: *1*	一	Additional Stroke: *3*	
_3_ **mian**	俛	Radical Stroke: *2*	Radical Seq: *3*	亻	Additional Stroke: *7*	
_3_ **mian**	兔	Radical Stroke: *2*	Radical Seq: *4*	儿	Additional Stroke: *5*	
_3_ **mian**	冕	Radical Stroke: *2*	Radical Seq: *7*	冂	Additional Stroke: *9*	
_3_ **mian**	勉	Radical Stroke: *2*	Radical Seq: *13*	力	Additional Stroke: *7*	
_1_ **mie**	乜	Radical Stroke: *1*	Radical Seq: *5*	乙	Additional Stroke: *1*	
_2_ **ming**	冥	Radical Stroke: *2*	Radical Seq: *8*	冖	Additional Stroke: *8*	
_4_ **mu**	募	Radical Stroke: *2*	Radical Seq: *13*	力	Additional Stroke: *11*	

M

			Radical	Radical		Additional
3	nai	乃	Stroke: **1**	Seq: **4**	丿	Stroke: **1**
2	**Nan**	南	Stroke: **2**	Seq: **18**	十	Stroke: **7**
2	**Nan +**	南	Stroke: **2**	Seq: **18**	十	Stroke: **7**
2	**men**	門	Stroke: **8**	Seq: **3**	門	Stroke: **0**
2	**Nan +**	南	Stroke: **2**	Seq: **18**	十	Stroke: **7**
1	**gong**	宮	Stroke: **3**	Seq: **10**	宀	Stroke: **7**
4	nei	內	Stroke: **2**	Seq: **5**	入	Stroke: **2**
3	ni	你	Stroke: **2**	Seq: **3**	亻	Stroke: **5**
2	**Ni**	倪	Stroke: **2**	Seq: **3**	亻	Stroke: **8**
4	ni	匿	Stroke: **2**	Seq: **17**	匚	Stroke: **9**
4	ning	佞	Stroke: **2**	Seq: **3**	亻	Stroke: **5**
2	ning	凝	Stroke: **2**	Seq: **9**	冫	Stroke: **14**
2	nong	儂	Stroke: **2**	Seq: **3**	亻	Stroke: **13**
3	nu	努	Stroke: **2**	Seq: **13**	力	Stroke: **5**

N

		Radical	Radical		Additional
³ **ou**	偶	Stroke: **2**	Seq: **3**	亻	Stroke: **9**
¹ **Ou**	區	Stroke: **2**	Seq: **17**	ㄷ	Stroke: **9**
¹ **qu**	區				

			Radical Stroke:	Radical Seq:		Additional Stroke:
2	**pai**	俳	**2**	**3**	亻	**8**
4	**pan**	判	**2**	**12**	刂	**5**
4	**pan**	叛	**2**	**23**	又	**7**
1	**pang**	兵	**1**	**3**	丶	**5**
2	**pang**	傍	**2**	**3**	亻	**10**
1	**bang**	傍				
4	**bang**	傍				
2	**pao**	刨	**2**	**12**	刂	**5**
4	**bao**	刨				
2	**pao**	匏	**2**	**14**	勹	**9**
4	**pei**	佩	**2**	**3**	亻	**6**
1	**pi**	丕	**1**	**1**	一	**4**
3	**pi**	仳	**2**	**3**	亻	**4**
4	**pi**	僻	**2**	**3**	亻	**13**
1	**pi**	劈	**2**	**12**	刀	**13**

P   **P**

¹ pi	匹	Radical Stroke: **2**	Radical Seq: **17**	匸	Additional Stroke: **2**
³ pi	匹				
² pian	便	Radical Stroke: **2**	Radical Seq: **3**	亻	Additional Stroke: **7**
⁴ bian	便				
¹ pian	偏	Radical Stroke: **2**	Radical Seq: **3**	亻	Additional Stroke: **9**
² piao	剽	Radical Stroke: **2**	Radical Seq: **12**	刂	Additional Stroke: **11**
¹ biao	剽				
¹ ping	兵	Radical Stroke: **1**	Radical Seq: **4**	丿	Additional Stroke: **5**
³ pou	剖	Radical Stroke: **2**	Radical Seq: **12**	刂	Additional Stroke: **8**
¹ pu	仆	Radical Stroke: **2**	Radical Seq: **3**	亻	Additional Stroke: **2**
² pu	僕	Radical Stroke: **2**	Radical Seq: **3**	亻	Additional Stroke: **12**
² pu	匍	Radical Stroke: **2**	Radical Seq: **14**	勹	Additional Stroke: **7**

Q								Q

_1_ qi	七	Radical Stroke: **1**	Radical Seq: **1**	一	Additional Stroke: **1**
_3_ qi	乞	Radical Stroke: **1**	Radical Seq: **5**	乙	Additional Stroke: **2**
_1_ Qi	亓	Radical Stroke: **2**	Radical Seq: **1**	二	Additional Stroke: **2**
_4_ qi	亟	Radical Stroke: **2**	Radical Seq: **1**	二	Additional Stroke: **7**
_2_ ji	亟				
_4_ qi	企	Radical Stroke: **2**	Radical Seq: **3**	人	Additional Stroke: **4**
_2_ qi	其	Radical Stroke: **2**	Radical Seq: **6**	八	Additional Stroke: **6**
_2_ chi	其				
_2_ qian	乾	Radical Stroke: **1**	Radical Seq: **5**	乙	Additional Stroke: **10**
_1_ gan	乾				
_3_ qian	倩	Radical Stroke: **2**	Radical Seq: **3**	亻	Additional Stroke: **8**
_1_ qian	僉	Radical Stroke: **2**	Radical Seq: **3**	人	Additional Stroke: **11**
_2_ qian	前	Radical Stroke: **2**	Radical Seq: **12**	刂	Additional Stroke: **7**
_1_ qian	千	Radical Stroke: **2**	Radical Seq: **18**	十	Additional Stroke: **1**
_1_ qian	仟	Radical Stroke: **2**	Radical Seq: **18**	十	Additional Stroke: **3**
_4_ qiao	俏	Radical Stroke: **2**	Radical Seq: **3**	亻	Additional Stroke: **7**

			Radical	Radical		Additional
2	qiao	僑	Stroke: **2**	Seq: **3**	亻	Stroke: **12**
3	qie	且	Stroke: **1**	Seq: **1**	一	Stroke: **4**
2	qie	伽	Stroke: **2**	Seq: **3**	亻	Stroke: **5**
1	jia	伽				
1	qie	切	Stroke: **2**	Seq: **12**	刀	Stroke: **2**
4	qie	切				
1	qin	侵	Stroke: **2**	Seq: **3**	亻	Stroke: **7**
2	qin	勤	Stroke: **2**	Seq: **13**	力	Stroke: **11**
1	qing	傾	Stroke: **2**	Seq: **3**	亻	Stroke: **11**
1	**Qing**	卿	Stroke: **2**	Seq: **20**	卩	Stroke: **8**
1	**Qiu**	丘	Stroke: **1**	Seq: **1**	一	Stroke: **4**
2	qu	劬	Stroke: **2**	Seq: **13**	力	Stroke: **5**
1	qu	區	Stroke: **2**	Seq: **17**	匚	Stroke: **9**
1	**Ou**					
4	qu	去	Stroke: **2**	Seq: **22**	厶	Stroke: **3**
3	qu	取	Stroke: **2**	Seq: **23**	又	Stroke: **6**

2 **Quan**	全	Radical Stroke: **2**	Radical Seq: **5**	入	Additional Stroke: **4**
4 **quan**	券	Radical Stroke: **2**	Radical Seq: **12**	刀	Additional Stroke: **6**
4 **quan**	勸	Radical Stroke: **2**	Radical Seq: **13**	力	Additional Stroke: **18**
4 **Que**	卻	Radical Stroke: **2**	Radical Seq: **20**	卩	Additional Stroke: **7**

R

			Radical	Radical		Additional
3	**Ran**	冉	Stroke: *2*	Seq: *7*	冂	Stroke: *3*
2	**ren**	人	Stroke: *2*	Seq: *3*	人	Stroke: *0*
2	**Ren**	仁	Stroke: *2*	Seq: *3*	亻	Stroke: *2*
4	**ren**	仞	Stroke: *2*	Seq: *3*	亻	Stroke: *3*
2	**Ren**	任	Stroke: *2*	Seq: *3*	亻	Stroke: *4*
4	**ren**	任				
4	**ren**	刃	Stroke: *2*	Seq: *12*	刀	Stroke: *1*
2	**reng**	仍	Stroke: *2*	Seq: *3*	亻	Stroke: *2*
3	**rong**	冗	Stroke: *2*	Seq: *8*	冖	Stroke: *2*
3	**ru**	乳	Stroke: *1*	Seq: *5*	乙	Stroke: *7*
2	**ru**	儒	Stroke: *2*	Seq: *3*	亻	Stroke: *14*
4	**ru**	入	Stroke: *2*	Seq: *5*	入	Stroke: *0*
4	**ruo**	偌	Stroke: *2*	Seq: *3*	亻	Stroke: *9*

R

			Radical	Radical		Additional
1	sa	仁	Stroke: 2	Seq: 3	亻	Stroke: 3
4	sa	卅	Stroke: 2	Seq: 18	十	Stroke: 2
1	san	三	Stroke: 1	Seq: 1	一	Stroke: 2
3	san	傘	Stroke: 2	Seq: 3	人	Stroke: 10
1	san	參	Stroke: 2	Seq: 22	ム	Stroke: 9
1	shen	參				
1	can	參				
1	cen	參				
1	**Seng**	僧	Stroke: 2	Seq: 3	亻	Stroke: 12
3	sha	傻	Stroke: 2	Seq: 3	亻	Stroke: 11
4	shang	上	Stroke: 1	Seq: 1	一	Stroke: 2
4	**Shang +**	上	Stroke: 1	Seq: 1	一	Stroke: 2
1	**Guan**	官	Stroke: 3	Seq: 10	宀	Stroke: 5
1	shang	傷	Stroke: 2	Seq: 3	亻	Stroke: 11
1	shan	刪	Stroke: 2	Seq: 12	刂	Stroke: 5
4	shao	劭	Stroke: 2	Seq: 13	力	Stroke: 5

S

2 **shao**	勺	Radical Stroke: **2**	Radical Seq: **14**	勹	Additional Stroke: **1**
2 **zhuo**	勺				
2 **She**	佘	Radical Stroke: **2**	Radical Seq: **3**	人	Additional Stroke: **5**
4 **She**	厙	Radical Stroke: **2**	Radical Seq: **21**	厂	Additional Stroke: **7**
2 **shen**	什	Radical Stroke: **2**	Radical Seq: **3**	亻	Additional Stroke: **2**
2 **shi**	什				
1 **shen**	伸	Radical Stroke: **2**	Radical Seq: **3**	亻	Additional Stroke: **5**
4 **sheng**	乘	Radical Stroke: **1**	Radical Seq: **4**	丿	Additional Stroke: **9**
2 **cheng**	乘				
4 **sheng**	剩	Radical Stroke: **2**	Radical Seq: **12**	刂	Additional Stroke: **10**
1 **sheng**	勝	Radical Stroke: **2**	Radical Seq: **13**	力	Additional Stroke: **10**
4 **sheng**	勝				
1 **sheng**	升	Radical Stroke: **2**	Radical Seq: **18**	十	Additional Stroke: **2**
4 **shi**	世	Radical Stroke: **1**	Radical Seq: **1**	一	Additional Stroke: **4**
4 **shi**	事	Radical Stroke: **1**	Radical Seq: **6**	亅	Additional Stroke: **7**
4 **shi**	仕	Radical Stroke: **2**	Radical Seq: **3**	亻	Additional Stroke: **3**

			Radical Stroke: 2	Radical Seq: 3	亻	Additional Stroke: 6
4	**shi**	侍	Radical Stroke: 2	Radical Seq: 3	亻	Additional Stroke: 6
3	**shi**	使	Radical Stroke: 2	Radical Seq: 3	亻	Additional Stroke: 6
4	**shi**	勢	Radical Stroke: 2	Radical Seq: 13	力	Additional Stroke: 11
3	**shi**	匙	Radical Stroke: 2	Radical Seq: 15	匕	Additional Stroke: 9
2	**chi**	匙	Radical Stroke: 2	Radical Seq: 15	匕	Additional Stroke: 9
2	**shi**	十	Radical Stroke: 2	Radical Seq: 18	十	Additional Stroke: 0
4	**shou**	受	Radical Stroke: 2	Radical Seq: 23	又	Additional Stroke: 6
4	**shu**	倏	Radical Stroke: 2	Radical Seq: 3	亻	Additional Stroke: 9
2	**shu**	叔	Radical Stroke: 2	Radical Seq: 23	又	Additional Stroke: 6
1	**shua**	刷	Radical Stroke: 2	Radical Seq: 12	刂	Additional Stroke: 6
4	**si**	伺	Radical Stroke: 2	Radical Seq: 3	亻	Additional Stroke: 5
4	**ci**	伺				
4	**si**	似	Radical Stroke: 2	Radical Seq: 3	亻	Additional Stroke: 5
4	**si**	俟	Radical Stroke: 2	Radical Seq: 3	亻	Additional Stroke: 7
4	**si**	兕	Radical Stroke: 2	Radical Seq: 4	儿	Additional Stroke: 5
1	**si**	厶	Radical Stroke: 2	Radical Seq: 22	厶	Additional Stroke: 0

4	**Sing**	信	Radical Stroke: **2**	Radical Seq: **3**	亻	Additional Stroke: **7**
4	**xin**	信				
1	**sou**	叟	Radical Stroke: **2**	Radical Seq: **23**	又	Additional Stroke: **8**
2	**su**	俗	Radical Stroke: **2**	Radical Seq: **3**	亻	Additional Stroke: **7**

1 ta	他	Radical Stroke: 2	Radical Seq: 3	亻	Additional Stroke: 3	
2 tan	倓	Radical Stroke: 2	Radical Seq: 3	亻	Additional Stroke: 8	
3 tang	倘	Radical Stroke: 2	Radical Seq: 3	亻	Additional Stroke: 8	
3 tang	儻	Radical Stroke: 2	Radical Seq: 3	亻	Additional Stroke: 20	
4 ti	俶	Radical Stroke: 2	Radical Seq: 3	亻	Additional Stroke: 8	
4 chu	俶					
4 ti	倜	Radical Stroke: 2	Radical Seq: 3	亻	Additional Stroke: 8	
4 ti	剃	Radical Stroke: 2	Radical Seq: 12	刂	Additional Stroke: 7	
1 ti	剔	Radical Stroke: 2	Radical Seq: 12	刂	Additional Stroke: 8	
2 tiao	佻	Radical Stroke: 2	Radical Seq: 3	亻	Additional Stroke: 6	
2 ting	亭	Radical Stroke: 2	Radical Seq: 2	亠	Additional Stroke: 7	
2 ting	停	Radical Stroke: 2	Radical Seq: 3	亻	Additional Stroke: 9	
2 Tong	仝	Radical Stroke: 2	Radical Seq: 3	人	Additional Stroke: 3	
2 Tong	佟	Radical Stroke: 2	Radical Seq: 3	亻	Additional Stroke: 5	
2 tong	侗	Radical Stroke: 2	Radical Seq: 3	亻	Additional Stroke: 6	
4 dong	侗					

2 **tong**	僮	Radical Stroke: **2**	Radical Seq: **3**	亻	Additional Stroke: **12**	
1 **tou**	偷	Radical Stroke: **2**	Radical Seq: **3**	亻	Additional Stroke: **9**	
4 **tu**	兔	Radical Stroke: **2**	Radical Seq: **4**	儿	Additional Stroke: **6**	
2 **tu**	凸	Radical Stroke: **2**	Radical Seq: **11**	凵	Additional Stroke: **3**	
2 **tuo**	佗	Radical Stroke: **2**	Radical Seq: **3**	亻	Additional Stroke: **5**	

			Radical	Radical		Additional	
2	**wan**	丸	Stroke: *1*	Seq: *3*	丶	Stroke: *2*
1	**wan**	剜	Stroke: *2*	Seq: *12*	刂	Stroke: *8*
2	**wang**	亡	Stroke: *2*	Seq: *2*	亠	Stroke: *1*
4	**wei**	位	Stroke: *2*	Seq: *3*	亻	Stroke: *5*
3	**wei**	偉	Stroke: *2*	Seq: *3*	亻	Stroke: *9*
3	**wei**	偽	Stroke: *2*	Seq: *3*	亻	Stroke: *9*
4	**wei**	偽				
4	**wei**	偎	Stroke: *2*	Seq: *3*	亻	Stroke: *9*
2	**Wei**	危	Stroke: *2*	Seq: *20*	卩	Stroke: *4*
3	**wen**	刎	Stroke: *2*	Seq: *12*	刂	Stroke: *4*
1	**wo**	倭	Stroke: *2*	Seq: *3*	亻	Stroke: *8*

W W

			Radical Stroke: 2	Radical Seq: 1	二	Additional Stroke: 2
3	**Wu**	五	Radical Stroke: 2	Radical Seq: 1	二	Additional Stroke: 2
3	**Wu**	伍	Radical Stroke: 2	Radical Seq: 3	亻	Additional Stroke: 4
3	**wu**	仵	Radical Stroke: 2	Radical Seq: 3	亻	Additional Stroke: 4
3	**wu**	侮	Radical Stroke: 2	Radical Seq: 3	亻	Additional Stroke: 7
4	**wu**	務	Radical Stroke: 2	Radical Seq: 13	力	Additional Stroke: 9
4	**wu**	勿	Radical Stroke: 2	Radical Seq: 14	勹	Additional Stroke: 2
3	**wu**	午	Radical Stroke: 2	Radical Seq: 18	十	Additional Stroke: 2

4 **xi**	係	Radical Stroke: **2**	Radical Seq: **3**	亻	Additional Stroke: **7**	
1 **xi**	傒	Radical Stroke: **2**	Radical Seq: **3**	亻	Additional Stroke: **10**	
1 **xi**	傌	Radical Stroke: **2**	Radical Seq: **3**	亻	Additional Stroke: **12**	
1 **xi**	兮	Radical Stroke: **2**	Radical Seq: **6**	八	Additional Stroke: **2**	
4 **xia**	下	Radical Stroke: **1**	Radical Seq: **1**	一	Additional Stroke: **2**	
2 **xia**	俠	Radical Stroke: **2**	Radical Seq: **3**	亻	Additional Stroke: **7**	
2 **xia**	匣	Radical Stroke: **2**	Radical Seq: **16**	匚	Additional Stroke: **5**	
1 **xian**	仙	Radical Stroke: **2**	Radical Seq: **3**	亻	Additional Stroke: **3**	
1 **Xian**	先	Radical Stroke: **2**	Radical Seq: **4**	儿	Additional Stroke: **4**	
3 **Xlan**	洗	Radical Stroke: **2**	Radical Seq: **9**	冫	Additional Stroke: **6**	
3 **xiang**	享	Radical Stroke: **2**	Radical Seq: **2**	亠	Additional Stroke: **6**	
4 **xiang**	像	Radical Stroke: **2**	Radical Seq: **3**	亻	Additional Stroke: **12**	
4 **xiao**	儌	Radical Stroke: **2**	Radical Seq: **3**	亻	Additional Stroke: **10**	
1 **xiao**	削	Radical Stroke: **2**	Radical Seq: **12**	刂	Additional Stroke: **7**	
4 **xue**	削					
1 **xie**	些	Radical Stroke: **2**	Radical Seq: **1**	二	Additional Stroke: **6**	

2 **xie**	偕	Radical Stroke: **2**	Radical Seq: **3**	亻	Additional Stroke: **9**
2 **xie**	協	Radical Stroke: **2**	Radical Seq: **18**	十	Additional Stroke: **6**
4 **xie**	卸	Radical Stroke: **2**	Radical Seq: **20**	卩	Additional Stroke: **6**
4 **xin**	信	Radical Stroke: **2**	Radical Seq: **3**	亻	Additional Stroke: **7**
4 **Sing**	信				
4 **xing**	倖	Radical Stroke: **2**	Radical Seq: **3**	亻	Additional Stroke: **8**
2 **xing**	刑	Radical Stroke: **2**	Radical Seq: **12**	刂	Additional Stroke: **4**
1 **xiong**	兄	Radical Stroke: **2**	Radical Seq: **4**	儿	Additional Stroke: **3**
1 **xiong**	兇	Radical Stroke: **2**	Radical Seq: **4**	儿	Additional Stroke: **4**
1 **xiong**	凶	Radical Stroke: **2**	Radical Seq: **11**	凵	Additional Stroke: **2**
1 **xiong**	匈	Radical Stroke: **2**	Radical Seq: **14**	勹	Additional Stroke: **4**
1 **xiu**	休	Radical Stroke: **2**	Radical Seq: **3**	亻	Additional Stroke: **4**
1 **Xiu**	修	Radical Stroke: **2**	Radical Seq: **3**	亻	Additional Stroke: **8**
4 **xu**	勖	Radical Stroke: **2**	Radical Seq: **13**	力	Additional Stroke: **9**
4 **xu**	卹	Radical Stroke: **2**	Radical Seq: **20**	卩	Additional Stroke: **6**
1 **xun**	勛	Radical Stroke: **2**	Radical Seq: **13**	力	Additional Stroke: **10**
1 **xun**	勳	Radical Stroke: **2**	Radical Seq: **13**	力	Additional Stroke: **14**

X

_1_ **ya**	丫	Radical Stroke: **1**	Radical Seq: **2**	丨	Additional Stroke: **2**	
_3_ **ya**	亞	Radical Stroke: **2**	Radical Seq: **1**	二	Additional Stroke: **7**	
_4_ **yan**	俺	Radical Stroke: **2**	Radical Seq: **3**	亻	Additional Stroke: **8**	
_3_ **an**	俺					
_3_ **yan**	偃	Radical Stroke: **2**	Radical Seq: **3**	亻	Additional Stroke: **9**	
_3_ **yan**	儼	Radical Stroke: **2**	Radical Seq: **3**	亻	Additional Stroke: **20**	
_3_ **yan**	兗	Radical Stroke: **2**	Radical Seq: **4**	儿	Additional Stroke: **7**	
_4_ **yan**	厭	Radical Stroke: **2**	Radical Seq: **21**	厂	Additional Stroke: **12**	
_3_ **Yang**	仰	Radical Stroke: **2**	Radical Seq: **3**	亻	Additional Stroke: **4**	
_2_ **yang**	佯	Radical Stroke: **2**	Radical Seq: **3**	亻	Additional Stroke: **6**	
_1_ **yao**	么	Radical Stroke: **1**	Radical Seq: **4**	丿	Additional Stroke: **2**	
_2_ **yao**	傜	Radical Stroke: **2**	Radical Seq: **3**	亻	Additional Stroke: **10**	
_2_ **yao**	僥	Radical Stroke: **2**	Radical Seq: **3**	亻	Additional Stroke: **12**	
_3_ **jiao**	僥					
_3_ **ye**	也	Radical Stroke: **1**	Radical Seq: **5**	乙	Additional Stroke: **2**	
_3_ **ye**	冶	Radical Stroke: **2**	Radical Seq: **9**	冫	Additional Stroke: **5**	

[1] yi	一	Radical Stroke: **1**	Radical Seq: **1**	一	Additional Stroke: **0**
[2] yi	一				
[4] yi	一				
[4] yi	义	Radical Stroke: **1**	Radical Seq: **4**	丿	Additional Stroke: **1**
[3] yi	乙	Radical Stroke: **1**	Radical Seq: **5**	乙	Additional Stroke: **0**
[4] yi	亦	Radical Stroke: **2**	Radical Seq: **2**	亠	Additional Stroke: **4**
[3] yi	以	Radical Stroke: **2**	Radical Seq: **3**	人	Additional Stroke: **3**
[1] Yi	伊	Radical Stroke: **2**	Radical Seq: **3**	亻	Additional Stroke: **4**
[4] yi	佚	Radical Stroke: **2**	Radical Seq: **3**	亻	Additional Stroke: **5**
[1] yi	依	Radical Stroke: **2**	Radical Seq: **3**	亻	Additional Stroke: **6**
[4] yi	佾	Radical Stroke: **2**	Radical Seq: **3**	亻	Additional Stroke: **6**
[3] yi	倚	Radical Stroke: **2**	Radical Seq: **3**	亻	Additional Stroke: **8**
[2] yi	儀	Radical Stroke: **2**	Radical Seq: **3**	亻	Additional Stroke: **13**
[4] yi	億	Radical Stroke: **2**	Radical Seq: **3**	亻	Additional Stroke: **13**
[4] yi	刈	Radical Stroke: **2**	Radical Seq: **12**	刂	Additional Stroke: **2**
[3] yin	尹	Radical Stroke: **1**	Radical Seq: **4**	丿	Additional Stroke: **3**
[4] Yin	印	Radical Stroke: **2**	Radical Seq: **20**	卩	Additional Stroke: **4**

Y
Y

4 **yong**	佣	Radical Stroke: **2**	Radical Seq: **3**	亻	Additional Stroke: **5**	
3 **yong**	俑	Radical Stroke: **2**	Radical Seq: **3**	亻	Additional Stroke: **7**	
1 **yong**	傭	Radical Stroke: **2**	Radical Seq: **3**	亻	Additional Stroke: **11**	
3 **yong**	勇	Radical Stroke: **2**	Radical Seq: **13**	力	Additional Stroke: **7**	
4 **you**	佑	Radical Stroke: **2**	Radical Seq: **3**	亻	Additional Stroke: **5**	
1 **you**	優	Radical Stroke: **2**	Radical Seq: **3**	亻	Additional Stroke: **15**	
4 **you**	又	Radical Stroke: **2**	Radical Seq: **23**	又	Additional Stroke: **0**	
3 **you**	友	Radical Stroke: **2**	Radical Seq: **23**	又	Additional Stroke: **2**	
2 **yu**	予	Radical Stroke: **1**	Radical Seq: **6**	亅	Additional Stroke: **2**	
3 **yu**	予					
2 **Yu**	于	Radical Stroke: **2**	Radical Seq: **1**	二	Additional Stroke: **1**	
2 **Yu**	余	Radical Stroke: **2**	Radical Seq: **3**	人	Additional Stroke: **5**	
2 **Yu**	俞	Radical Stroke: **2**	Radical Seq: **3**	人	Additional Stroke: **7**	
3 **yu**	傴	Radical Stroke: **2**	Radical Seq: **3**	亻	Additional Stroke: **11**	
2 **Yuan**	元	Radical Stroke: **2**	Radical Seq: **4**	儿	Additional Stroke: **2**	

Y **Y**

1 **yuan**	冤	Radical Stroke: **2**	Radical Seq: **8**	宀	Additional Stroke: **8**		
2 **Yuan**	原	Radical Stroke: **2**	Radical Seq: **21**	厂	Additional Stroke: **8**		
4 **yue**	刖	Radical Stroke: **2**	Radical Seq: **12**	刂	Additional Stroke: **4**		
2 **yun**	云	Radical Stroke: **2**	Radical Seq: **1**	二	Additional Stroke: **2**		
3 **yun**	允	Radical Stroke: **2**	Radical Seq: **4**	儿	Additional Stroke: **2**		
2 **yun**	匀	Radical Stroke: **2**	Radical Seq: **14**	勹	Additional Stroke: **2**		

¹ **za**	匝	Radical Stroke: **2**	Radical Seq: **16**	匸	Additional Stroke: **3**	
⁴ **zai**	再	Radical Stroke: **2**	Radical Seq: **7**	冂	Additional Stroke: **4**	
² **zan**	偺	Radical Stroke: **2**	Radical Seq: **3**	亻	Additional Stroke: **9**	
⁴ **ze**	仄	Radical Stroke: **2**	Radical Seq: **3**	人	Additional Stroke: **2**	
² **ze**	則	Radical Stroke: **2**	Radical Seq: **12**	刂	Additional Stroke: **7**	
⁴ **zha**	乍	Radical Stroke: **1**	Radical Seq: **4**	丿	Additional Stroke: **4**	
⁴ **zhai**	債	Radical Stroke: **2**	Radical Seq: **3**	亻	Additional Stroke: **11**	
⁴ **zhan**	佔	Radical Stroke: **2**	Radical Seq: **3**	亻	Additional Stroke: **5**	
⁴ **Zhan**	占	Radical Stroke: **2**	Radical Seq: **19**	卜	Additional Stroke: **3**	
¹ **zhan**	占					
⁴ **zhang**	丈	Radical Stroke: **1**	Radical Seq: **1**	一	Additional Stroke: **2**	
¹ **Zhang**	仉	Radical Stroke: **2**	Radical Seq: **3**	亻	Additional Stroke: **2**	
⁴ **zhang**	仗	Radical Stroke: **2**	Radical Seq: **3**	亻	Additional Stroke: **3**	
⁴ **zhao**	兆	Radical Stroke: **2**	Radical Seq: **4**	儿	Additional Stroke: **4**	
¹ **zhen**	偵	Radical Stroke: **2**	Radical Seq: **3**	亻	Additional Stroke: **9**	
¹ **zhi**	之	Radical Stroke: **1**	Radical Seq: **4**	丿	Additional Stroke: **3**	

Z   Z

			Radical	Radical		Additional
2	**zhi**	值	Stroke: **2**	Seq: **3**	亻	Stroke: **8**
4	**zhi**	制	Stroke: **2**	Seq: **12**	刂	Stroke: **6**
1	**zhi**	卮	Stroke: **2**	Seq: **20**	卩	Stroke: **3**
1	**Zhong**	中	Stroke: **1**	Seq: **2**	丨	Stroke: **3**
4	**Zhong**	中				
4	**Zhong**	仲	Stroke: **2**	Seq: **3**	亻	Stroke: **4**
4	**Zhong +**	仲	Stroke: **2**	Seq: **3**	亻	Stroke: **4**
1	**Sun**	孫	Stroke: **3**	Seq: **9**	子	Stroke: **7**
3	**zhong**	冢	Stroke: **2**	Seq: **8**	宀	Stroke: **8**
4	**zhou**	冑	Stroke: **2**	Seq: **7**	冂	Stroke: **7**
3	**zhu**	主	Stroke: **1**	Seq: **3**	丶	Stroke: **4**
4	**Zhu**	住	Stroke: **2**	Seq: **3**	亻	Stroke: **5**
4	**zhu**	佇	Stroke: **2**	Seq: **3**	亻	Stroke: **5**
1	**zhu**	侏	Stroke: **2**	Seq: **3**	亻	Stroke: **6**
4	**zhu**	助	Stroke: **2**	Seq: **13**	力	Stroke: **5**

Z

			Radical	Radical		Additional
4	**zhuan**	傳	Stroke: **2**	Seq: **3**	亻	Stroke: **11**
2	**chuan**	傳				
3	**zhun**	准	Radical Stroke: **2**	Radical Seq: **9**	冫	Additional Stroke: **8**
2	**zhuo**	勺	Radical Stroke: **2**	Radical Seq: **14**	勹	Additional Stroke: **1**
2	**shao**	勺				
2	**Zhuo**	卓	Radical Stroke: **2**	Radical Seq: **18**	十	Additional Stroke: **6**
3	**zi**	仔	Radical Stroke: **2**	Radical Seq: **3**	亻	Additional Stroke: **3**
3	**zong**	偬	Radical Stroke: **2**	Radical Seq: **3**	亻	Additional Stroke: **11**
3	**zu**	俎	Radical Stroke: **2**	Radical Seq: **3**	人	Additional Stroke: **7**
2	**zu**	卒	Radical Stroke: **2**	Radical Seq: **18**	十	Additional Stroke: **6**
4	**cu**	卒				
4	**zui**	最	Radical Stroke: **2**	Radical Seq: **7**	冂	Additional Stroke: **10**
3	**Zuo**	佐	Radical Stroke: **2**	Radical Seq: **3**	亻	Additional Stroke: **5**
4	**zuo**	作	Radical Stroke: **2**	Radical Seq: **3**	亻	Additional Stroke: **5**
4	**zuo**	做	Radical Stroke: **2**	Radical Seq: **3**	亻	Additional Stroke: **9**

Z

Z